P9-CAY-455

SMART

DANE ZELLER

SHIELD

One Monkey Typing™
Westwood, Kansas
www.danezeller.com

ISBN: 978-0-9848867-0-8
ISBN-10: 0-984-88670-2

One Monkey Typing
One Monkey Typing and the Monkey Finger Logo are Trademarks of One Monkey Typing

For Rita

Acknowledgements

The Wednesday Thursday Friday writing group: Many thanks to my friends Bob Chrisman, Kerry Hubbard, Teresa Vratil, Dawn Downey, Jessica Conoley, and Karin Frank.

The Kansas City Writers Group: The group that moves me along to my writing goals: Mike Lance, Wes Crenshaw, Pam Eglinski, Theresa Hupp, Maril Crabtree, Peg Nichols, Anton Jacobs and so many others who, with a few compliments, corrections, recommendations, push my writing towards excellence.

My Friend: Thanks to Greg Hodes, for his subtle critique and enthusiastic support.

Chapter 1

The Kansas Highway Patrol forced the silver Lincoln to the side of the interstate five miles west of Topeka at 3:00 a.m. Oncoming traffic was light. The spotlights on the patrol car lit up the suspect's vehicle through the light rain. The driver, a black man, remained motionless.

"Run the plate. See if he's our guy."

"A 2008 Town Car."

"That's him."

" He's wanted for questioning in Edwardsville. Two off-duty cops shot dead at a bar. It's an armed and dangerous."

"Uh oh."

"Let's get him away from his car. We don't need any chase in this weather."

The officers stepped out of their cruiser and took up positions behind their doors, with guns drawn. The patrolman on the driver's side keyed the mic: "Open your door, and step slowly out of the car."

The driver's door opened, and one leg, then the other, swung out onto the wet pavement.

"Did you call for backup?"

"Yeah."

"We can't wait for 'em. Just be careful. Watch him."

The large man dressed in gray slacks and a black jacket stood up and faced the officers. His left hand was at his side, but his right hand was chest high.

"Both arms *up*."

A flash from the motorist's left hand was met immediately by four shots from the police revolvers. The suspect crumpled to the pavement.

They slowly approached the man on the ground, with their guns still pointed at him. "I think he's dead."

"Jesus."

"We had no choice. He drew on us."

"Damn, he's dead, I know he's dead."

"He was armed and dangerous, for God's sake. We followed procedure."

"Yeah, I know, but...geez."

"I think his gun slid under the car. You look for it. I'll check his ID."

One patrolman dropped down next to the Lincoln and swept his hand under it to search for the gun. The other checked the man's pulse.

The officer searching for the weapon stood up with an object in his hand.

"I've got no pulse. What do you have?"

"Uh...partner...I got a badge."

"A badge? But, I saw the flash from the barrel."

"I did too. What the hell?"

"Well, here's his gun. It's in his holster."

"We didn't shoot a cop."

"Yeah, we did. His ID says he works for the Kearney, Missouri police department."

"Aw shit."

" His name is John Friend."

He looked up at his partner.

"He's their Chief of Police."

Chapter 2

Trucks and trailers and other heavy equipment filled the lighted yard the size of a city block. A guard shack in one corner provided security for the assets of a large Kansas City corporation. The shell of a six story building overlooked the yard from the north. Remnants of the stockyards stretched out to the west.

"Don... Don."

"Uh...yeah, yeah, what's up?"

"What's up? Not you, for sure. You missed gate three and gate four on the half hour."

"No, I got'em."

"No, Don, you didn't. You were asleep," Don's supervisor said.

"I was resting my eyes. I'm on it."

" Sorry, Don. I've got to have someone more reliable. I'm taking over. Get your things."

Don Milkey stood up and took a brown corduroy sport jacket off the back of the chair. When he put it on, he pulled on the front as if to button it. A few wrinkles subsided, but the button fell short of the button hole. He reached for a paperback on the desk, revealing a frayed cuff of his coat. He crowded the novel into his back pocket.

Don moved a pen and a few sheets of paper into the desk drawer and tossed a Styrofoam coffee cup into a trash can.

He shook his supervisor's hand. "I appreciate the opportunity."

"You got some drool on the front of your shirt."

Don looked down and wiped it away.

"You know random checks at the entry points are better than scheduled checks..." Don said.

"Yeah, yeah, put it in your next textbook."

"Call me if you get in a bind," Don said.

"Sure, I'll have Jesus call you."

Milkey left the complex and headed to the parking lot. He approached his black 1998 Ford Crown Victoria on the passenger side, opened the door and slid across behind the wheel. The driver's window was down a half inch, allowing the light rain to collect on the sill inside the car. Don pushed the button on the armrest, but the window didn't move.

He drove out of the West Bottoms, heading for his apartment on the east side of downtown. At the Sixth and Broadway overpass, a homeless man worked the traffic. His sign read, "Need money for food." Down below, the interstate buzzed under a series of bridges that provided shelter for the man and his colleagues. Don stopped and squeezed four quarters through the gap in his window. As the man took the money and God-Blessed him, Milkey noticed the man's shoes. They were ecco brand shoes, retail price, about 600 quarters.

Don parked in front of the brick building and walked up three flights of stairs. The door opened into the kitchen with full view of the living room that served as a bedroom. A carton of Chinese food sat on the kitchen counter. Noodles spilled over onto the surface. A piece of chicken had dropped onto the floor. He went to the window where he looked into the distance to see the interstate turning north, crossing the river and heading to the suburbs.

The green light blinked on his answering machine on the end table.

Beep.

"Hey, Don, this is Bill down at the print shop. Thought I'd call you about that thirty dollars you owe on that last batch of business cards. It's getting a little old. Come on down and we'll have some coffee. Bring your wallet. Hah, hah."

Click.

Don took off his uniform shirt, opened the refrigerator, brushed aside an aging bunch of celery, and grabbed a soft drink. He stooped to pick up the piece of chicken and then tossed it into the trash can.

Beep.

"Don, this is Frank. We missed you at the last meeting. Hope everything's going all right. You've got my number if you need any help. God loves you, and so do I."

Click.

Beep.

"This is David at Security Northwest. It's ten o'clock. I was expecting you to be on duty at 9:30. Give me a call, so I know if I have to get a sub. "

Click.

Beep.

"Dinner's at 1:00 this Sunday. Please be on time. See you."

Click.

Beep.

"Hi Don, this is Helen. Miss you. Give me a call."

Click

Beep.

"Uh...Mr. Milkey, I met you at the Security Convention in St. Louis last month. We traded cards. We talked about cops and P.I.'s helping each other out. But, that's not why I'm calling. I...I got a problem. I need to speak to you in person. Call me at 816...uh...well, just call me at the number on my card. Please, I need to talk to you right away. My name's John Friend."

Click.

Chapter 3

The noon sun shone through Don's apartment window and onto his feet. The midday heat did not rouse him from his sleeping position in the recliner.

"...please, Mr. Milkey, I can't stand this. I can't do this on my own."

Click.

Don awoke. He looked around the apartment. He looked at his watch and then at the answering machine. The green light was blinking again. He wound the tape back to the start of the message.

"Mr. Milkey, I'm calling you about...about...my husband. I don't know who to turn to. John gave me your business card before...before...he left last night."

Her voice lowered in volume and steadiness. Don turned up the machine.

"Someone is...was...after my husband. "

The tape continued to turn, but no words came out, just the sound of labored breathing.

"They...they killed him last night."

Don moved closer to the speaker. The sobs were muffled.

"Please call me. I don't know what to do. Call me on this number, not the one on his business card. My name is Portia."

"...please, Mr. Milkey, I can't stand this. I can't do this on my own."

Click.

Don picked an audio tape out of the end table drawer. He removed its wrapper, opened the answering machine and switched tapes. The old one went into his pocket. He put on a shirt, combed his hair, and left the apartment.

He walked three blocks to a local convenience store. Its windows were barred, the parking lot trashed. An old, but shiny, Lincoln Continental filled a parking slot on the side of the building. Three rows of food and sundries filled the store. Some of the cans and boxes were coated with dust. Refrigerated cases, well-stocked with beer, lined the back wall.

"Hey, Cap'm," the burly man behind the cashier's gate said.

"Hi, Jackson," Don said.

"Find any bad guys lately?"

"Nah, I'm between contracts right now."

"Heard you were doing some guard work down in the bottoms."

"Yeah, well that's one of those contracts I'm between." Don grinned. "Is that all you got for cereal, just corn flakes?"

"Cap'm, check it out, we ain't the Piggly Wiggly."

"You'd think after everyone bought the corn flakes, you'd bring in some grape nuts."

"We ain't got room for tastes of all cultures in the neighborhood."

"I'm just asking for something new."

"I'll order a big box for you, general."

"Thanks for the promotion."

"That it, just the corn flakes and milk?"

Don looked over Jackson's shoulder at the cell phones hanging on the rack.

"I need one of those cell phones. Are they all 816 numbers?"

"Yeah. That what you need?"

Don paused. "No."

Jackson sacked up the corn flakes and milk.

"That'll be seventy-six eighty."

Don pulled a hundred dollar bill from his wallet.

Jackson counted out the change, put the receipt in the bag, and pulled a cell phone from beneath the counter and put it in the bag.

"What's the area code?"

"Don't know, Cap'm."

"Thanks Jackson, you're my favorite store."

Don picked up his bag and started out of the store.

"Cap'm Milkey."

"Yeah?"

"You my PI, ain't you?"

"Yup."

"Then we got that confidentiality thing going, don't we?"

"I got your back."

"I know that."

Don dialed Portia Friend's number on his way back to the apartment.

" Mrs. Friend?"

"Oh thank goodness."

"I'm sorry to hear about your husband."

"They called it an accident. He was shot by Kansas Highway patrolmen. They thought he was involved in a killing. But, Mr. Milkey, someone was after him. It wasn't an accident. John told me to call you if anything happened to him."

"Mrs. Friend, we need to meet. The number I just called, is it your home phone?"

"It's a cell phone. I just bought it from Wal-Mart. You're the only one with the number. I thought people might try to listen in."

"You must have arrangements to make. Call me when you're able to meet with me."

"Mr. Milkey, my husband was just killed. You better believe I've got arrangements to make. I need to see you as soon as possible."

"Where are you?"

"Liberty."

"How about the Wal-Mart on Highway 150?"

"Yes, when?"

"Three o'clock, in the Subway inside the store."

"I'll be there. Thank you, Mr. Milkey. Thank you so very much."

"Don't worry, Mrs. Friend. We'll get to the bottom of this."

Chapter 4

Don parked his Crown Vic in the employees' lot behind Central High School. Helen approached with a smile, and jiggled the passenger's door handle. Don reached over to unlock the door, but it was already unlocked. She bent over and looked into the car at Don, pointing at the door lock. She jiggled it again. Don smiled. She tried again and it opened.

She slid into the passenger seat and leaned over to kiss him. "Were you worried?"

"About the door not opening? No. I knew it was...what do you call it...your...?"

"Crown Vic humor," she said. "I've got great material."

"Don't make fun of my car. I paid nine hundred for it."

"I'm not making fun of your car. I'm making fun of you."

"I feel better, then."

"Don, I got you a present." She opened a sack that had "Nordstrom's" printed on the side.

"You got me a present from Nordstrom's?"

"Are you kidding me? I got the sack from the school secretary. I got your new tie from my neighbor's garage sale. It's just your color, barbeque sauce red. Get it?"

"Yeah. Should I put it on now?"

"Why rush your makeover?" Helen opened another sack that came from Walmart. "I got me a new shirt. It's an antique. Look. No, don't. Keep your eyes on the road. It's got an old gas pump in front of a tiny gas station. It says 'Up Your Ass With Mobilgas'. Whatdya think?"

"I think there wouldn't be many places you could wear that."

"Casual Fridays at school."

"In front of those impressionable young students?"

"They wouldn't notice. Hey, I've got an idea. Let's go buy you a new car. Whatdya say?"

"I can't. They'd ask me if I was employed."

Helen looked at Don. "You're not a security guard anymore?"

"They didn't like how I did it."

"Piss on 'em. There's other fish in the sea, ducks on the pond, birds in the hand."

"I'm comforted by your clichés."

"Who're we meeting? she asked.

"The wife of the Kearney Chief of Police."

"Stop there. I see it all. He's cheating on her and she wants evidence for that big honking divorce settlement. I can smell your fee already. Maybe I can do my shopping at a real store now. Right?"

"Not quite. Kansas State Highway patrolmen shot him dead last night."

"Oh, my god. Are you shittin' me? How'd that happen?"

Don shrugged.

"How did you get involved?"

Don related Portia's telephone call.

"Geez. And she's wanting to talk about it today?"

"Yup, she does."

"How can I help?"

"I don't know...I just thought...I'm not too good at..."

"Speaking, smiling, crying, nurturing, commiserating, talking, asking questions?"

"No."

"Comforting someone who's lost a loved one?"

"Yeah, that's it."

Don pulled his new cell phone from one pocket and the answering machine tape from another. He slid them both over to Helen.

"Would you find the number of the phone?"

Helen put the tape into her purse and took out a pen and piece of paper. She opened the phone, hit some keys, and then wrote down the number twice on the piece of paper. She tore the sheet in half and gave one half to Don and the other went into her purse.

"You've got some voice mail on your new phone, Don. Four messages."

"Let's hear' em."

Helen hit a button and held the phone to her ear. Don could hear the screaming.

"You son-of-a bitch. You set foot into my yard ever again and you'll get both barrels of daddy's shotgun, I swear I don't care if I go to jail for a million years, you bastard. You just enjoy that sweet young thing, and next time you screw that slut, you be thinking about those two 12 gauge shells I got loaded and where I'm going to be aiming next time I see you. Good-bye you mother-fucker."

Beep.

"And another thing you cheating bastard, I got your car keys. Don't be counting on your car being there where you left it. Someday, you'll come out of her apartment with one less car, you asshole. Good fuckin' bye.

Beep.

"Get a lawyer and grab your left nut, you jerk-off, you're in for a fight."

Beep.

"You fuckin' mother-fucker. So long."

"You need a different cell phone supplier, Don. Want to erase them?"

"Yep."

"Might be a case in here down the road."

"Erase 'em."

Chapter 5

The Crown Vic crossed the river, heading north to Liberty. Don swerved across two lanes of traffic and exited on the 210 Highway ramp. Drivers left behind on the interstate shook their fists and extended their fingers after slamming on their brakes to avoid hitting Don's car. The blue Taurus was caught in the middle of the traffic, not able to exit. The driver did not gesture.

"Did we shake him?" Helen asked.

"I think so," replied Don.

In the Wal-Mart store, the black woman sat at a table in the Subway. She wore a dark blue suit with light cream scarf peering from underneath her collar. The color her purse matched her scarf. Don and Helen approached her.

"You're Mr. Milkey," Portia said. She stood up, her tears welling in her eyes.

"Yes. Please call me 'Don', and this is my partner, Helen."

Portia grasped his extended hand with both of hers. Her tears turned to sobs. Don raised his other hand to place it on her shoulder, but Helen beat him to it with an engulfing hug.

"I've just got to be strong like John, but it's so hard."

"You will be, you will be," Helen said.

Portia regained her composure and the three of them took seats at the table.

"Portia, John left a message on my answering machine saying he wanted to talk with me. What was that about?"

"It started with a parking ticket he got in St. Louis at the convention, you know, the one where he met you. He parked on the street downtown and fed the meter. He thought it'd be cheaper than a parking lot. The meter went over time, about five minutes, and he got a parking ticket. He sent a check in when he got back, but a second parking ticket showed up the next week. Then, a third. He had seventeen parking tickets in the next four weeks. At first, he thought it was funny. He called St. Louis to complain about the tickets, but they only had a written record of one traffic ticket. They checked their database, and found the other sixteen tickets. They said there also was a warrant out for his arrest for auto theft, and there wasn't anything they could do about it, but they recommended he turn himself in. "

"Did he identify himself as a chief of police?"

"No."

"Did your husband ask if they could identify the source of the violations?"

"They said 'couldn't', but John thought it was 'wouldn't'."

"Then what'd he do?"

"He called his old boss in Kansas City, Captain Cassidy."

Don sighed.

"He's the guy who ran John out of the department, but he was the highest rank he knew down there."

"What'd Cassidy say about the tickets and the warrant?"

"He said for John to come down and they'd do some research together. John set up a time, but he didn't go. It was after that call that John believed someone was after him. "

"Someone?"

"Yes, someone in law enforcement. He said he couldn't trust anyone. He even wondered about his own force."

Don paused in his questioning. An older couple sat down at the table next to them.

"Mr. Milkey, John thought someone was after him. I know...I knew him. I was married to him for twenty years. John didn't jump to conclusions. If he thought someone was after him, then someone was. "

"Would that include his second-in-command?"

"It could."

"What's his name?"

"Bob Billingsley."

"When did you talk to him last?"

"At two this afternoon."

"What'd he tell you?"

"Oh, Mr. Milkey, we're in trouble. The guy is either behind this, or he's out of his league. The Kansas Highway Patrol is considering it an accident, and are closing the case. This guy isn't getting after anything."

Don turned to Helen.

"What's missing?"

Helen thought for a minute. "John called you, so your number would appear in his cell phone history. An investigator would be calling all the numbers in the history, but they haven't called you. That means someone is either not doing an investigation, or they are, and they don't want you involved in it."

Milkey surveyed the entrance of the Subway, and then glanced at the Wal-mart exit beyond the restaurant. " I need you to keep in touch with Billingsley. You need to push him. Take notes, and I'll call you in the morning. Can you do that?"

"I can."

Don got up, followed by Helen and Portia.

"Portia, we're leaving the store now, you stay a few minutes and then leave."

"Okay."

"We'll find out who's behind this."

"I know you will."

"Call me anytime if you need anything. You don't have to wait until the morning."

"Ok, Mr. Milkey."

"Please, call me 'Don'."

Chapter 6

"Portia is lucky," Helen said, as they settled in the car.

"How so? She just lost her husband."

Helen looked over at Don behind the wheel. A tear tracked down her cheek.

"She's got you."

"I don't know, I just lost a security guard job."

"I'm sorry I laughed at you."

"That's okay, I got over it."

"It took four days of not calling me for you to get over it."

"I've gone four days before without calling you."

"Not this kind of four days. This was: 'I-just-proposed-marriage-to-my-girlfriend-and-she-laughed-at-me' kind of four days."

"Nah, I was busy."

In the parking lot behind Helen's school, Don walked her to her car. She grabbed his hand on the way. When they reached her car, she kissed him. As they parted, their hands slipped their grip. Helen's were the last to let go.

A blue Taurus occupied a space in front of his apartment building. Don pulled up behind the car and then gunned the Crown Vic, smashing into the back of the smaller car. He jumped out and ran forward to inspect the damage. No damage to his car, but there was a dent in the Taurus bumper and the taillight was smashed.

"I'm sorry, I'm sorry." Don yelled. A man in his mid twenties stepped out of the car, his Chicago Cubs baseball cap on backwards. He walked to the back of his car.

"Don't worry, I've got insurance," Don said. "I'll call the police."

"No. That's not much damage. No problem."

"Let me get your name and insurance information. I'll give you mine," Milkey said.

"Hey, you know what? I've got to be somewhere in ten minutes, and this is a company car. It's old and they won't know or care about it. Let's just forget it."

The young driver hurried back to get in his car, and when he reached for the door handle, Milkey already had his hand on it. When the young man turned to look at Milkey, Don's face was six inches from his. "I don't know who you work for, and I don't care." Milkey leaned closer. "I have a job to do. Don't get in my way."

He let go of the handle and walked away. "Have a nice day."

"Yes, sir," the young man said.

Chapter 7

Don and Helen parked on the street in front of his sister's house. All the other cars were in the driveways in this southern part of Kansas City. Don knew Jeanne would worry about oil dripping onto her concrete driveway. All of the driveways were made of concrete on her block. None had oil stains.

"I'm happy you could make it to Sunday dinner, Helen," Jeanne said.

"Thanks for inviting me. I'm reeling from the changes they're making at the school. I needed a diversion and some of your famous fried chicken."

" Even on a Sunday you reel, away from work?"

"I do. Can't stop it."

"Well, here, have some mashed potatoes to help you forget your worries."

"Thanks, Jeanne. When I told Don I was dating him for his money, he told me he didn't have much, but he said he had a sister who could fry chicken like my Grandma. That was good enough for me, eh, Don?"

Don nodded in agreement, with his mouth full.

"What's Mobilgas?" the seventeen-year-old asked.

"Jake."

"It's an old brand of gasoline. Thanks for noticing my new shirt," Helen said.

"Jake, some brussels sprouts?"

"No thanks, Mom."

"Yes thanks, Jake."

He took one.

"Three"

"Two." Jake took two more.

"One more thing, Jake."

"What, mom?"

"Your cap."

"Oh yeah, do you like my Rockies cap?"

"Yes, but no one knows the name of the team. It's on backwards."

"Oh, my fault." He turned the cap around.

"Great." Jeanne said. "Now that everyone knows your affiliation, it doesn't need to be on your head anymore."

"Oh, yeah." He removed his cap. "Uncle Don, you got any secret investigations going on?"

Jeanne interrupted. "Honey, I thought I told you, your uncle is helping design a security system for the General Mechanics Corp. "

"Jeanne, I'm afraid that job ended."

"Oh?"

"Yup. We had a disagreement about how it was going to work. They wanted a system where guards would periodically visit checkpoints and punch a button. I told them they might as well post a schedule on the main gate."

"Did you recommend a camera system, Uncle Don?"

"Jake."

"Yes I did. They thought it'd cost a lot, and they'd have to wire the buildings."

"Wireless, Uncle Don. And they could get their cameras down at Wal-mart."

"They still thought they'd have to hire people to watch the screens."

"One person could monitor a hundred screens," Jake said. "All you need is some software to detect movement on the screens."

"Oh?" Don said. "They have that?"

"I don't know, but, think about it, the picture on the screen is digitized. If the screen changes from one second to another, all you'd need is a comparison each second to see if the digits have changed. That's nothing in programming. We're in the 21st century, Uncle Don. If you can imagine it, it's been done, or someone is working on it."

"Dang, Jeanne, when I was seventeen, I was an expert on lipstick colors, and types of mascara," Helen said.

"I wish Jake was an expert in history, biology and English. His report card would be better balanced," replied Jeanne.

Don turned to Jake. "I'm interested. Would you research that for me, that motion-detecting software?"

"Sure, Uncle Don. And get this: you could guard all of the General Mechanics complex from, let's say, Salt Lake City."

"Or, Mumbai."

"Yep."

"Like uncle, like nephew," Jeanne said.

"Can I be a researcher in your PI agency?" asked Jake.

"Jake, please," his mother said.

"Sure, but I'm refurbishing my office right now. You'd have to work at home, and...you'd have to learn history and English, too.

"It's a deal," Jake said.

"When's that office going to be finished?" Helen asked.

"That's the same question I asked my architect," Don said. "Jake, your first job will be to research laptops. I need quality and low price. Or, maybe just low price."

"Will you be doing anything beyond internet? Like movies and music?"

"No. It'll be just a communication device"

"Should I look nationwide?"

"I need it tomorrow."

"Ok. I'll text you tonight."

"I've got a new phone number." Don handed Jake the number for the phone he bought from Jackson.

The Crown Vic started and Don circled the cul-de-sac.

"Don." Helen paused. "Please be careful with Jake. I know it's a great thing for you two to have something in common, and I think it's okay for him to help you with technology things, but, you're working on a murder case. You gotta keep him out of that."

"He's seventeen."

"Don."

"Okay."

"Okay, what?"
"I won't involve him in the case."

Chapter 8

The words reverberated throughout the Homicide department, 2nd floor, police headquarters.

"Turn that damn hat around. You look like some college punk," said Captain Cassidy.

"It's part of the job, looking like a college student, not an undercover cop," the young man said.

"Look around you, Sean, are you in the street, or are you in my office?"

"Your office."

"Then have some respect for your boss. Now where'd Milkey go?"

"He went to Central High and picked up a lady."

"Okay, and then what happened?"

"Then...then, I don't know where they went."

"Shit. You lost him? How'd that happen?"

"He was in the left lane of I-29, and then crossed over two lanes of traffic and took an exit."

"You didn't do the same?"

"I wanted to live."

"Don't get smart with me, rookie. I'm your boss. Your career's in my hands. Did you go back to Central High and wait?"

"No, I went back to his apartment building."

"When did he get back?"

"About 5:00 pm."

"Did he see you there?"

"No." Sean answered with no discernible pause.

"Good. I want surveillance on him all day tomorrow. I want a report by 7:00 P.M."

"Will do."

Sean stood up to leave Cassidy's office. "What's up with this Milkey guy?"

"It's just preventative. We've got an investigation going on, and we're making sure he's not going to interfere with it."

"What investigation is that?"

"Sean, you concentrate on handling the little things, like keeping your cap on straight. Leave the big things to me."

"Yes, sir."

Chapter 9

Billingsley turned in his chair, and gazed out the large plate glass window of the corner office that overlooked downtown Kearney, Missouri. It was a big office, easily accommodating the 6 foot 4 inch, two hundred seventy-five pound lawman.

"A Mr. Milkey to see you, Chief."

Billingsley reached over to the telephone on the corner of the expansive desk and pushed a button.

His voice boomed: "Tell him I'm in a board meeting for about three hours. Be glad to see him about four this afternoon."

The door opened, and Milkey peered inside. "Oh, I was looking for the john."

"It's right down the hallway to the left."

"Thank you sir, I hope I didn't interrupt anything."

"No problem."

"Wait, aren't you Captain Billingsley?"

"Yes, I am."

Don opened the door wider and entered the room with his hand outstretched.

"I'm Don Milkey, a private investigator working for Portia Friend."

"Pleased to meet you, Mr...ah..."

"That's 'Milkey,' like the candy bar."

Don quickly scanned the office, then took in the view from the window.

"Great day we're having, and what a view you've got from here. Mind if I ask a few questions about the shooting of John Friend?" asked Don.

"Well, not much to tell. Kansas has done the work on it. Looks like an accident, a very unfortunate accident involving a couple of good patrolmen over there."

"Why'd they pull John over?"

"I think he had a few traffic tickets."

"Sounds unusual for them to be watching for someone with a few parking tickets."

"Well, I'm not sure their procedure. You never know what some patrolman will do if they see a black man out at 3:00 am, I'm afraid to say. They might have an interest. Now we don't do any of that in my district, but you don't know how they do it in other jurisdictions."

"Was there a warrant out for him?"

"There might of been. Kansas is handling that. They'll check into it."

Don edged over to a photograph hanging on the wall next to the plate glass window.

"Must've been some fishing trip. Looks like at least forty fish you guys are holding."

"Yeah, that was back in '92. Bunch of us went up into Canada."

"Portia told me there was a warrant out for his arrest a week ago for auto theft."

"John would've told me about that."

"Did he tell you about the tickets?"

"Yeah, he did, but he didn't say he had a bunch of them."

"Tell me, Captain, how'd he get shot?"

"As I understand it, when he exited the car, he was holding something that flashed, and the patrolmen fired. Turned out he was showing his badge."

"The patrolmen had their guns at the ready?"

"I imagine so. Listen Mr. Mabee, I'm needing to get to a meeting right now; is that all you wanted?"

"Well, I've got a few more questions."

"Check with my secretary and set up an appointment, for say, next week?"

"I'll do that." Don moved toward the door. "Thanks for your help. I know Portia will appreciate any help you give us."

"I'm happy to help. John'll be sorely missed in our community."

Don eased out the door, but turned around.

"One more thing, Chief. It's been awhile since I've been on a force. Is it customary nowadays to have a motorist exit a car during a traffic stop, let's say for parking tickets?"

"You got a point there. I'm not sure how they do it over in Kansas. We'll talk next week."

"I'll set it up with your secretary."

Don closed the door with the brass name plate on it that said "Chief Friend."

Chapter 10

Intermittent showers blew past the conference room on the eighth floor of the Jefferson Building in downtown Denver. A photo appeared on the screen.

"This is Brent Iverson, CEO of Innovative Solutions. He is the genius behind this organization, and was the one who put the team together. Don't be fooled by his young looks. You'd guess he's in his early twenties, but he's 37.

"The next slide is that of Thornton Hopkins, our chief of security. He worked for the National Security Agency for thirty years before he joined us. He looks to be in his mid-fifties, doesn't he? I assure you, he's all of that."

Chuckles came from the ten or twelve people at the table. A hand raised. "How does his experience apply to the software you're selling. If I purchase Smart Shield and install it in my bank, all I want is to keep hackers out. What's NSA got to do with that?"

"Good question," The presenter said. "Not only does Thornton provide security for Innovative Software during our product's development, but his skills at NSA are appropriate in the design of the software. The mission of NSA is both code breaking *and* code making."

The next slide showed a man in his early forties, with a silver streak down the middle of his black hair. "This handsome man is Paul Mazzoli, vice-president of marketing"

Mazzoli moved in front of the screen next to the digital Mazzoli. "Do you see the resemblance?"

Laughter came from the group at the table.

"On this next slide is a picture of Dr. Kevin Rathbone, perhaps the world's leading authority on computer security. He is a graduate of Carnegie-

Mellon University. He has taught at MIT. Frankly, he's the reason I agreed to come on board. Before we even designed our product, I knew Dr. Rathbone and his five engineers would produce a stone-wall security system. And they did. As you get to see Smart Shield operate, and become familiar with its features, you are going to see one beautiful system. We are indeed fortunate to have Dr. Rathbone as part of the development and maintenance teams here at Innovative Solutions. If you choose to go with our system, you will enjoy the company of a brilliant man."

Down the hall, and around the corner from the conference room, Thornton Hopkins, head of security, leaned forward in his chair at the desk of Brent Iverson, CEO.

"He's gone? Whatd'ya mean he's gone?

"Rathbone and I had a disagreement. He threatened us. I threatened him. He quit and then left," Iverson said.

"Just like that? We lost our team leader because you guys had a squabble?

"He detected a bug in the software and wanted to shut down all five installations. I told him we could fix it on the fly, and keep the customers running. He was insistent."

"I thought I told you I needed to be in on all important decisions."

"He made the decision, not me."

"Well, shit, Brent."

"We were going to lose him anyway. Besides, the bug he was talking about was the extra code we installed. I think he discovered he wasn't in complete control of development."

"Find him."

"I'll try. But we can get by without him. We were going to let him go sometime."

"I'm not worrying about getting by without him. I'm worrying about him talking. Get him back."

Chapter 11

Don parked his car in front of his apartment building. A man dressed in coveralls shouted at him from the porch. "Sir, you no park in handicap parking."

Don did not reply as he walked up the sidewalk.

"How you hanging, my friend?" the man on the porch said.

"How you doing, Garcia?"

"I'm hanging fine, chief."

"Did you get my garbage disposal working?"

"No sir, I'm busy patching roof."

"By the way, Garcia, that 'How are you hanging.' shouldn't be used to greet women."

"No for women? I do not use for women."

"Helen said you did, the last time she came over."

"Oh, your girlfriend, yes, I remember. She say it first."

"First? I'll have to talk to her about that. She knows I'm teaching you etiquette."

"But she no park in handicap spot."

"Look at the street, Garcia. Are there any other open places?"

"No sir. But you break law."

"No, Garcia. Are there any handicapped people living in our building?"

"No, but..."

"So, no harm, no law broken."

"No hablo American law," Garcia said.

"By the way, 'How are you hanging is an old greeting. It tells people you're at least fifty-five years old."

"I'm thirty-five. People no see my face? They listen to words to tell?"

"They pay attention to all of the clues. What you say, and how you say it, tells much about you."

Don reached in his pocket, pulled out a twenty dollar bill and gave it to Garcia.

"Please look out for strangers who come up to the building."

"Like blue Taurus with broken tail light and dent in rear bumper?"

"He was here today?"

"Yes. He left 15 minutes ago."

"What did the driver look like?"

"He was young guy with baseball hat on backwards."

"You're a good investigator, Garcia. Could you fix my garbage disposal, too?"

"Yessir. Did you want to know about the van?"

"The van?"

"White, tinted windows, new cargo van. It parked across the street. No one get out. They were here three hours."

"What makes you think they were looking for me?"

"Ah, Mr. Milkey, we just little criminals here. We don't need new fancy vans. There is big reason this van wait here. They big people doing big things. They looking for you. You are important."

"Keep your eye out for me, Garcia."

"Yessir, Chief."

"And don't call me 'Chief'."

"Okay, Chief."

Don walked up the stairs to his apartment. He looked closely at the lock, unlocked the deadbolt, and entered. He went over to the living room window and checked the lock on the window. It was secured. He went over to his recliner and looked at his answering machine on the end table. There were three messages on it. Don picked up the machine and turned it over. There was a bulge under a piece of tape. He slowly removed the tape, went into his bathroom and taped the device under the toilet tank

Chapter 12

Well, you wake up in the morning, hear the ding-dong ring... Don's cell phone rang.

"Mr. Milkey, this is Portia Friend."

"How's it going, Portia."

"Not well, Mr. Milkey. I just talked to Billingsley, and he's not doing nothing about nothing. He's not trying. God almighty, I thought I was through with this. If John was white, Billingsley would be all over this case. I'm going there at 3:00 this afternoon. Come on over if you don't mind a little shouting."

"Portia, Portia, ease on down, now. I'll be there. Three o'clock."

"That's right, Mr. Milkey, the show starts at 3:00. Don't be late or that police department will be solving another crime right there in his office."

"I'll be there."

At 2:58 pm, Don Milkey walked up to the receptionist at the Kearney Police department. He started to say something to her, but he was interrupted by the sounds coming from Billingsley's office.

"How long did it take you to move into the big dog's office, huh? It's like you were measuring the room for new furniture before you even knew what happened to John."

The sound of something breaking accompanied Portia's tirade.

"Have a seat," said the receptionist. "I'll see if the chief... Captain Billingsley is available."

Don followed her to the door of the chief of police. She opened it. Billingsley was standing up behind his desk with his arms stretched out in front of him.

"Now, now, Mrs. Friend, calm down. Let's talk about this."

"We done talking, Billingsley. Now we'll be doing."

"We're working on it, Mrs. Friend. We just can't force the highway patrol to move faster. Tell her, Milkey, we've got to follow procedure on this."

Portia moved closer to Billingsley. "He works for me, he isn't telling me nothing. I want to know who put those sixteen parking tickets on John's record, who put the auto theft warrant on it, and why you won't find out."

Billingsley looked over at Milkey.

"Help me here, Milkey."

"Like she says, I work for her. She's mad. I'd do what she says."

"You damn straight."

Portia rummaged through her purse. She found an envelope and handed it to Milkey.

"There's a thousand. I got more. You'd think my tax money would be working on this, but that ain't the case. I guess this one's on my tab. I'm leaving now. Mr. Milkey, you know what to do."

Portia left without looking at Billingsley.

"Wow, I haven't seen a black woman that mad before," said Billingsley.

"You're accustomed to seeing a white woman that mad?"

"Well...uh...you know what I mean."

"No, I don't. She just lost her husband, and you're sitting in his chair behind his desk. She's pissed, whatever her color. She wants to know who fed the sixteen traffic tickets into the national database, who put in the warrant for his arrest on auto theft, and, I might add, what else is on his record."

"Well, Milkey, as I've told you, Kansas is working the case, and I'll let you know as soon as possible."

"I've got an idea. Let's just boot up your computer here on your desk and peer into that database."

"I...I don't have the password."

"How about your old office. You got a computer there and a password?"

"Yes, but. Well, I'll tell you this. You realize you're just a private investigator, I mean, you're a civilian, and I've got to maintain security and all, and I just can't be showing you information that is private, especially when it could affect the family of a victim."

" Billingsley, listen to yourself. I represent Portia Friend, the widow of the man whose seat you occupy. Did you just hear what she said? She wasn't interested in privacy, Captain. She wanted the information. Now I'm going to ask you a question, and if you can't answer it, I'm going to take this envelope full of money and maybe put some more with it, and I'm going to find the answer myself. You don't know me, but perhaps you've heard about me. If I've got a reputation out there, it ain't for following the rules. As I investigate, as I do my work for Portia Friend, I'll be scouring all the corners of this case, and the results won't be a pretty picture, and I can't say you won't be in the snapshot. Now, I'm asking you, who put the sixteen traffic tickets in the national database? And 'I don't know,' isn't an answer."

Billingsley shifted his attention from Don to the computer on his desk. He opened the desk drawer, gave a cursory glance inside, and then shut it. He looked at Don.

"Milkey, let me explain. Whenever we, or any law enforcement agency, log into the database system, it logs our user name and checks our password. If we log in to add a person or a ticket to the system, it records our username. Every single record in that database has a username affixed to the violation, except for sixteen traffic tickets affixed to John Friend's record. I'm afraid to say it, but my answer is: 'I don't know the answer'."

Chapter 13

...you're in trouble with the man...

"Uncle Don, this is Jake."

"Hey, did you find me a computer?" Don asked.

"Did you want a netbook or a laptop."

"Laptop."

"Micro-centre on Metcalf, a Toshiba Satellite, $459, or you can go on-line for it for $399."

"Thank you. I'd rather pick it up today and spend the extra sixty bucks."

"Thirty. You'd have shipping."

"Even better. Say, Jake, you said you'd like to do some research for me?"

"Sure, I'd love to."

"I'm interested in the national and state databases that law enforcement use to distribute information on criminals and violations."

"You want me to hack into them?"

"No, I'm just looking for their websites."

"No problem. I'm on it."

"And Jake, you need to let your mother know what you're doing. Maybe you don't have to be real specific about what you're doing for me, but you've got to talk to her about it."

"I'll tell her I'm researching crime-fighting tools."

"And don't ignore your history homework."

"Okay, the history of crime-fighting tools."

"No, Jake, I know you love computers. Just spread the love to your other school subjects."

"Will do, Uncle Don. I'll call you tomorrow."

Chapter 14

Portia exited I-29 at the Liberty turnoff. She drove the frontage road to a new housing development. She turned on Douglas Street and then finally into the driveway of the house at 14432. The double garage door lifted, and Portia parked the little Toyota on the right hand side. She gathered her purse and the box of John's personal belongings and crossed the empty left side of the garage.

She entered the kitchen and was met by Pong, the black cat she had purchased the week after they found their first cat shot to death in their front yard. She rubbed up against Portia's leg.

Portia opened the cupboard above the sink. She unscrewed the lid of a coffee container and dumped the contents on the counter. She counted the money: a hundred ninety, hundred dollar bills. On a piece of paper she wrote '19,000' and put it in the container along with the bills. The doorbell rang. Portia quickly capped the container and placed it back on the shelf.

At the door stood a woman holding a box. She didn't say anything. Portia hesitated. Then the woman said, "Portia...I...I didn't know what to do. So, I made a meatloaf." She held out the box to Portia. Portia reached for the box with one hand, and embraced the woman with the other.

"Thank you, Kathy, thank you so much."

The two women hugged for a few more minutes.

"Want to come in?"

"No, Portia, I can't. I can't just now. I'm sorry. I'm sorry."

They hugged one more time before Kathy turned away and walked towards the house directly across the street.

From her purse, Portia retrieved her new cell phone and dialed Milkey's number.

"Mr. Milkey, I want to apologize for the scene I caused in Billingsley's office."

"I didn't think anything about it, Portia. I thought you were quite appropriate."

"Before you got there, Billingsley referred to you as 'Mr. Milkey', but one time he started out with 'Captain.' Are you a captain?"

"Not now, but a long time ago I was a police captain. All that's behind. Just call me 'Don.'"

"Did he have anything to say after I left?"

"Yes. He said all entries in the database require a source. Your husband's sixteen records did not have a source. He could not explain why not."

"Could not or would not?" Portia asked.

"I think 'could not'. I judge him to be incompetent, not evasive."

"I wouldn't be so sure, but thank you for all you've done for me. I'm stronger now; maybe you picked up on that. You don't know how much you've helped me, Mr. Milkey."

Chapter 15

Steam rose from the grate. One person in a sleeping bag was near the heat source, but did not touch it. Make-shift blankets of rags, newspapers and cardboard covered all the others, keeping the cool morning air at bay. At 7:00 in the morning, one man boiled a mixture of water and coffee grounds over a can of Sterno he had pulled from a bag that had 'Salvation Army' printed on the side.

The man thumbed through a stack of signs and picked the one that said 'Veteran needs work or food. God Bless you.'

A high-pitched voice came from one of the piles of blankets and cardboard.

" That you Bikerman?"

"Yeah."

"Thanks for trading with me. Now I got morning rush tomorrow, right?"

"Yeah."

"Wanna mix our take?"

"Yeah."

"Tomorrow's the last day of the week. It'll be better than today. That's why we should mix it. Okay?"

"Yeah."

"Good luck. You better be goin' now. You'll miss the crowd, if you don't."

"Yup."

Bikerman walked up the embankment to the bridge.

The sleeping bag moved.

"Hey, Kevin, you awake?"

"Lulu, shut up. I can't sleep with you jammerin'," someone beneath a pile of papers said.

"I'm awake," Kevin said.

"You wanna go with me to the 8th street bridge this noon? We'll go as a family. That'll work. I'll make up a new sign. Somethin' about our whole family losin' our jobs."

No response from the sleeping bag.

"How 'bout it, Kevin?"

"Nah."

Chapter 16

Paul and Cathy's Cafe sat midway between the Kansas State House and the Highway Patrol Headquarters in Topeka. The patrons associated with lawmaking wore suits; those who enforced the law wore uniforms. However, only a few customers were at the cafe at 9:00 A.M., including one young man dressed in jeans and a polo shirt. His face was shaved clean, and his hair cut short. The waitress was pouring him coffee when Milkey took a seat across from the younger man. Don flashed a badge.

"I'm Don Milkey. I'm doing some work for the Kearney, Missouri Police Department."

The man's gaze lowered, and so did his shoulders.

"How did you know I was involved?"

"I was sitting in the back, and I waited for those who weren't on administrative leave to exit the cafe. You were left."

"You're good. How long you been with them?"

"Not long." said Don. "I'm the rookie doing the grunt work. You don't mind me asking a few questions? I was headed to your department to pick up your report on the shooting, but I thought I might find you here."

"No problem. There's an internal investigation going on, but I can talk about anything in my police report."

"I can't say I know what you're going through," Don said. "But I had a teenager draw a gun on me once. I had half a second to tell if it was a real or fake pistol. I chose fake. I was right, but I could've easily been in the shoes you're in today."

"Or dead."

"Right, or dead. My new chief told me this Friend guy had something in your database."

"Yeah, he had a lot of parking tickets, but we were looking for a Lincoln involved in a hold up in Eudora."

"So you were looking for the car."

"Yeah. And when we saw it, we pulled it over. I ran the plate and got a shitload back on the guy, including auto theft, and the holdup showing two cops killed."

"What'd you do?"

"Well, you've been there before. Our sphincter meter pegged, and we stepped out of the car with guns drawn and ordered the guy out of his car. He came out, hands up. My partner and I saw a flash from one hand, and we let loose. We didn't wait to find out what was in his hand. We just shot. I've thought about this a lot since I pulled the trigger. I...I... can't believe I could have done anything else. We're trained. They move, we react. Time is life, we're told. I wish I could have it back, but I can't. Now I'm sitting here in my civilian clothes, and I can't go into the department to do my job...and...this guy...Friend...is dead."

"Did you hear any shots?"

"Are you kidding me? We were reacting; we weren't observing. Hell, right after he went down, I thought I heard twenty shots, but turned it was only four. When the investigation is over, we'll be cleared. I know that. We followed procedure. I'll have my job back, and that will be great. But no internal report is going to take away that moment I found the badge under the Lincoln. Right now, I see that badge about ten, twenty times a day. As time goes on, that will go away, but not completely, I suspect."

The young patrolman's stare was fixed on his coffee cup. He maintained his focus and grip on the cup until Don reached over and poked his hand. The young patrolman looked up.

"That's the cost of doing something important," Don said.

The officer nodded.

Don gathered some change from the table, leaving some for a tip.

"Thanks for talking with me. My chief appreciates your help."

"You're welcome. Glad to help."

"One more thing. When you brought him up on your computer, what did you see?"

"I saw a whole lot of parking tickets. Four of them were unpaid and flagged for a warrant. He had a warrant for auto theft. And he was wanted for a hold up in Eudora, where two local cops were shot and killed."

"I didn't read anything in the newspaper about cops being killed."

"They weren't. I called Eudora ten minutes after we left the scene. No one on their force had been killed."

"And the holdup?"

"None. You know, when bad things happen to us, we try to protect ourselves by saying that shit happens. I'm trying to use that now, and it ain't working."

"I don't understand."

"When I was making my report, I looked back at the database. Every entry in the file has a source tagged to it. If you got a speeding ticket in Salina, the source would be Salina P.D. I checked with a friend I have down at the municipal court in town. He says anytime they enter a violation, it requires a registered agency source code. He says you can't have a violation record without one."

"Your point?"

"Friend's entries had blanks for their source. Shit didn't happen to John Friend. Someone was after him. Someone smart."

Chapter 17

Milkey parked his car in front of his apartment building, grabbed his new computer from the passenger seat, and stopped by his mailbox. There were six envelopes from credit card companies, a letter from the National Security Guard Forum, a hand-addressed regular sized envelope with no return address, and a bulky envelope with an address label affixed at an angle. When he reached his kitchen table, Don tossed the credit card envelopes into the trash. The bulky envelope contained a CD, a flash drive, and a typewritten note. "Call me when you get your computer."

No signature.

"Did you get your computer, Uncle Don?"

"Yeah. And I got your CD and flash drive, too."

"Good. Any questions?"

"Nope."

"I've got some," Jake said. "Are you using the computer on a case?"

"Yup."

"Then you want some protection. The CD has a copy of a brand name virus detection program. The problem with it is that it contacts its own website for file updates, and it does it often. I disabled that function. They don't know you've got it, but then, you won't be getting the latest updates. That's okay, for a while."

"Is that legal, Jake?"

"Legal? I don't know. But don't worry about that. It's a bootleg version anyway; now that's illegal."

"I was afraid of that."

"Who's your internet provider?"

"I don't have one."

"Good. It's better that you don't. On the CD is a wireless signal detector, a good one. If you don't want anyone to know who you are, it's best you use someone else's' service. Maybe someone has a wireless router in your building."

"Traceable to someone in my apartment building?"

"Could be."

"I don't want that."

"Then you're stuck with McDonald's, Starbucks, and anyone else you drive by who's got an unsecured signal.

"That would be inconvenient, but necessary."

"And, Uncle Don, the flash drive is a computer on a stick. It has a Linux operating system, a browser, a suite of office tools, virus protection and encryption capabilities. You can use the flash drive and piggyback on most computers as long as they'll boot from a flash drive."

"Not sure why I'd need that, but I'll keep it in mind. Find out anything about the crime databases?"

"I'm working on it. And, Uncle Don, don't put anything on your computer that's related to your name or phone number. Don't buy anything on it. Don't sell anything on it. When you create an e-mail name, make sure it doesn't mean anything. Don't use 'crimefinder' or 'privateeye'."

"Your mother needs to know what you're doing. You're helping me set up a secure computer, right?"

"Don't worry, Uncle Don."

Milkey opened the last envelope. He pulled out a photo showing twelve men posing for a camera shot. They had fishing equipment and strings of fish. He had seen this photo before. The second man from the left was Billingsley. There was no note, no marks and nothing written on the envelope.

Chapter 18

The photo lay face up on the Subway table, in front of Mrs. Friend.

"I only know Billingsley," said Portia, handing the photo back to Milkey.

Helen sipped on a medium-sized Dr. Pepper.

"What do you think, Helen. What do you see?" Don lowered his voice as an employee cleaned a nearby table.

"I see twelve white men, ranging in age from thirties to fifties. They have money, if that lake is in Canada, and I think it is. The fishing equipment is not Wal-mart, it's Bass-Pro, expensive line."

"What else?"

"It's the photo in Billingsley's office," Portia said.

"And you don't recognize any of these faces? There's no one there from the Kearney police department?" Don asked.

"No, and no one from the town, "Portia said. "Maybe guys from K.C. That's where he came from."

"I don't recognize anyone, but that was years ago," Don said. "What's missing here, Helen?"

"Someone sent you a message. Someone who can't speak to you directly. They know something."

"It's pretty high definition," Don said. "Most likely, it was generated by a computer file, not a copy machine."

"So that would be someone with access to his computer files," Helen said. "Somebody in the department."

Don placed the photo back into the envelope, and the trio left the Wal-mart.

"I'll be right with you," Don said to the other two.

Don walked across the parking lot and up to the blue Taurus that was facing the front door of the store. A young man with a cowboy hat sat behind the wheel. He rolled the window down.

"Good afternoon," Don said.

"Good afternoon, sir," the young man replied.

Don opened the envelope and handed the photo to the man.

"Do you recognize anyone here?"

"The cowboy looked closely at each man's face.

"No, sir."

Don reached in and took the photo back.

"The cowboy hat attracts too much attention. It's a billboard that says, 'I'm not an ordinary guy.' Don't wear a hat," said Don.

"Thanks for the advice."

"No problem."

Milkey climbed the stairs to his apartment. Garcia was on his floor, replacing a light bulb.

"Afternoon, boss."

"How's it going, Garcia?"

"It's goin' great, partner."

"Are you looking out for me?"

"Yes sir, I see no Taurus and no van today."

Don handed him the photo.

"Look closely at these men's faces. Try to remember what they look like. If you see any of them around here, tell me."

Garcia slowly scanned the photo. He gave it back to Milkey.

"Uh, partner, you didn't ask me if I know any of these men," Garcia said.

"Oh, I guess I made an assumption there, Garcia. Do you know any of these men?"

"No." He smiled.

"Good job, you'll make a good private investigator."

"I'd be a good dick."

Don laughed.

"That's a word I have to be careful?"

"Yes."

"Jackson, do you have any milk that hasn't expired?" asked Milkey.

"Now there you go Cap'm, you thinkin' about suburban milk. This here is ghetto milk; you add two weeks to the expiration date here."

"And that makes it fresh?"

"Like a baby's bottom."

"I'm not sure that's a good comparison."

"Sure is. Now, what makes you think I know any of these crackers in this photo, pardon my French, Cap'm."

"I'm just making wild guesses, Jackson. I'll try anyone when I'm desperate. No Grape Nuts today?"

"I've got some fresh eggs in the cooler."

"I'll bet they're fresh."

Jackson rung up a loaf of bread, peanut butter, and a quart of milk.

"That'll be $12.75 today, Cap'm."

"Why don't you just hold a gun to my head?"

"What'd a discount store be doin' in the ghetto, Chief?"

"Because your customers don't have much money?"

"Thanks, Cap'm. Oh...and have a nice day. Isn't that what they say in the suburbs?"

"You got it," Don said, as he lifted the bag.

"Don't forget your photo."

"Oh, thanks, I almost forgot."

Don opened the door of the quick shop.

"Cap'm?"

Don stopped.

"You my PI, ain't you?"

"That's right."

"And what's said in the ghetto store, stays in the ghetto store?"

"If that's what you want."

Jackson stepped out from behind the cash register and glanced down the few aisles of his store. No one else was there.

"Second guy from the left, he's a cop. He called Billingsley. Time ago, he's in my store plenty, and he don't buy no milk fresh or no. Next to him is Butler. Don't know his first name. But I know'em both. Butler some big dog pooh bah in Springfield, Missouri. He's not a cop and no one in the picture besides Billingsley is a cop."

"That all?"

"No cap'm."

"What else?"

"Billingsley. He be fishin' with the Klan."

Chapter 19

"Thank goodness, you got rid of that damn hat," said Cassidy. "What's going on with Milkey?"

"Nothing out of the ordinary. He gets groceries at a quick stop in the ghetto."

"Jackson's?"

"Yeah, he bought something at an electronics store."

"What'd he buy?"

"Don't know."

"Well, was it as big as a TV? or smaller than a radio?"

"I'd say about the size of a DVD player."

"You don't know shit. Damn, where were you in training?"

"Milkey was at the Kearney police department yesterday."

"Who'd he see.?"

"I don't know."

"Didn't you get out of your car?"

"Uh, no."

"Geezus, you need to take some action. Find out something. He's at Kearny. Did he talk to Billingsley?"

"I expect he did."

"I don't assign you to expect things. I assign you to know things."

"Yes, sir."

"Now, how do you find out what he bought?"

The young man paused.

"You need to go through his fuckin' trash, you moron. Have some imagination. Check out what he's been charging on his credit card."

"You mean check out his credit card while he's under surveillance?"

"Hell, we're not building a case here, we're just getting information. We check his credit card *because* he's under surveillance."

"Yes, sir."

"Have you changed cars?"

"No, I'll do that tomorrow."

"I don't want him knowing we're on his ass."

"Yes, sir."

Chapter 20

Jeanne paused at the doorway to her son's bedroom.

"Jake, honey, did you get your history homework done?"

"Ah...not yet. I got an extra day."

"Are you doing work for Uncle Don?"

"Yes."

"And what would that be?"

"It's classified, mom."

"The hell."

"Relax, mom, it's a joke. I found him a computer."

"I worry, Jake. I don't know everything your uncle's doing. Who knows what enemies he's made."

"Don't worry, mom. I'm just a gopher researcher."

"Don't forget your homework."

"I won't."

"Uncle Don."

"Jake."

"I found the sign-in to some databases."

"Great, now all I need is a username and password."

"That'd be helpful," said Jake.

"Helpful, but not altogether necessary?" asked Don.

"Right."

"Tell me."

"Theoretically, you could find anyone's username and password. The user name is usually some variation of their real name. Say Bob Smith has the pin number or password 983533. You guess at the username, maybe bsmith or smithb, then run a program that increments the password by 1 until it reaches 983533."

"Won't it stop at three tries and lock you out?"

"Normally. But there's ways around that. Usually, after you've made the first attempt, a code becomes attached to the following attempts."

"So, you get rid of the code?"

"That's one way. Another is to revisit the log-in page, perhaps with a different browser, or even a different operating system."

"They can do that nine hundred-eighty-three thousand times?"

"Uncle Don, that's a small number."

"How do you know all this?"

"Simple. You can know this too. If you can imagine a solution to a problem, then someone in the world is working on it, or has already done it."

"I'm afraid my imagination in the technology world is limited."

"That's why you hire an assistant."

"Hire?"

"Okay, engage."

"So where's the imagined computer program?"

"You've got it. It's on the flash drive. The program will ask you for a person's name, phone number, street address, and alma mater. Don't worry, you'll get prompts."

"Jake, it's important to me for this to be okay with your mom. You giving me this program isn't a big deal. But, if you used the program, that'd be different. Understand?"

"Right, uncle Don, I'm researching tools, not people."

"That's correct."

Chapter 21

Milkey parked his car next to a new Ford Crown Victoria at the Kearney Police Station. Don looked over the blacked unmarked vehicle, and then back at his. The police car's driver-side window was more than halfway down, and the car had spotlights, too.

Inside the building a young man and woman sat in the reception area of the station. They talked in hushed tones, writing on note pads.

"Good morning, Mr. Milkey," the receptionist said. "We've met before, but we haven't been introduced. I'm Sarah Klein, office manager for Chief Friend."

"Friend?"

"Oh, I'm sorry. Chief Billingsley. Things happen too fast around here for me. At my age, speed kills."

"I understand."

"Please have a seat."

Sarah pressed a button on her phone. "Chief, don't forget your appointment with the *Star*."

"I'll be right out."

Ten minutes later, Billingsley walked out of his office and approached the two reporters. He did not look at Milkey.

"Good morning," Billingsley said. "Bob. Bob Billingsley." He smiled.

The three went into his office. Sarah offered coffee to the two visitors. They declined.

"Coffee, Mr. Milkey?"

"No thanks."

"I don't have you down for an appointment."

"Nah, I thought I'd just drop by."

"Hopefully this meeting won't last long."

"How long have you worked here, Sarah?"

"Twelve years."

"So you knew Chief Friend pretty well."

"I did."

"Pretty good chief?"

"No." Sarah said, as she glanced through a file folder. "Pretty good man."

"I'm sure Billingsley will work into the position."

"I'm sure," Sarah said, without looking up.

Milkey waited an hour for the meeting to break up. It did not.

"Those are reporters?"

"Yes," Sarah said.

"Doing a story on John, no doubt."

"No, Mr. Milkey, if that were the case, they'd be talking to me, too."

"They're not?"

"They're not.

Don looked closely at Sarah's face.

"Thanks for the photo."

No change. No pause in her work. No different expression.

"What photo?"

"The fishermen."

Sarah opened another file folder on her desk

"I don't understand."

Milkey didn't explain.

The meeting lasted two hours. They emerged from his office.

"Well, if I can help you any more, you've got my number. Give me a call." Billingsley smiled and walked them to the door.

Billingsley turned and walked back to his office. His smile was gone.

"Mr. Milkey's here to see you Chief."

Billingsley closed the door to his office without responding.

"I'm sorry, Mr. Milkey. You came all this way not to talk with him."

"That's okay. I enjoyed our chat."

Don opened the door to leave.

"Mr. Milkey."

Don stopped and looked back at Sarah. "Yes?"

Sarah's smile changed the path of the tear rolling down her cheek. "You're welcome."

Chapter 22

"...ain't no food upon the table and no pork up in the pan..."

From his bed, Don patted the top of a dresser drawer until he found his cell phone. "Hello."

"Hi honey. Is it too early to call?" Helen asked.

"It's noon," Don said.

"So?"

"I'm up."

"Have you read this morning's paper?"

"I don't get the paper anymore, Helen. You didn't know that?"

"Not exactly. I knew your paper was getting stolen. Remember? You accused Garcia of taking it and using it to brush up on his English."

"Yeah. I cancelled the subscription. He was always one step ahead of me on current events. I couldn't stand that. So what's the paper say?"

"Says the Chief of Police of Kearney, Missouri, is dead."

"I think we knew that. They're late to that party."

"I wouldn't jump to that conclusion."

"Whatdya mean?"

"Billingsley is dead."

"Huh?"

"He killed himself. In his office. At his desk. He'd talked to reporters from the *Star*. They were asking about his association with some racial hate groups. Apparently, he couldn't face an upcoming story."

"Damn."

"Did you suspect he was a racist?"

Don paused.

"Don?"

"I had some information about some Klan members being in that photograph in Billingsley's office."

"Who gave you that?"

"I promised I wouldn't say."

"You don't trust me?"

"It's not a matter of me trusting you. It's him trusting me. I promised him I'd protect him. Don't take it personal."

"Would you share it with your wife?"

"Yup."

" I'm kinda your partner. I could help you better if I had all the facts."

"You'll be the first to know."

Chapter 23

Milkey's Subway office was deserted, except for Don, Helen and Portia.

"I knew it, I knew it," Portia said.

"What do you know?" Don said.

"Billingsley was a racist."

"And...?"

"And what? He was a racist."

"That doesn't mean he killed your husband."

"It does, if Billingsley had a deal with the highway patrolmen."

"I talked with one of the patrolmen. He felt sorry for the shooting."

"He told you that, and you believed him?" Portia said.

"I've interviewed bad guys in my life. The guilty talk about themselves, reasons, alibis, and their luck. This patrolman talked about the shooting. And then he talked about the shooting some more. He was searching for some way he could've done it different. Portia, he killed your husband by accident."

"Okay, Mr. Milkey, I'm gonna believe you on this."

"What now?" Helen said.

"Let's talk about what we know," Don said. "John worked for Kansas City, and so did Billingsley."

"And John was edged out of the department," added Portia."Probably because he was black."

"Maybe so. Billingsley followed John to Kearney, and the only thing separating Billingsley from Chief of Police would be your husband's impeccable record. Billingsley needed a scandal. Some charges would help. He alters the database somehow to stir the pot. He couldn't foresee that John would be stopped and killed as a result, but, no doubt, it cleared the way for his promotion."

"It makes sense," Portia said.

"Except for one small thing," Don said.

"The Taurus is still on our tail," Helen said.

"No. It's a Crown Vic now, and it's out in the parking lot as we speak. It's the same kid. Somebody still thinks the case is open."

"Maybe they didn't get the word about Billingsley's suicide," Helen said.

"I don't know. I'm wondering about this tail. I talked to the kid the first time he tried to follow us. I told him to keep out of my way. Think about it. Proper procedure would be to report our conversation to his supervisor, and someone else would show up the next day. I think he didn't report it, that's why he's still the one tailing us. Someone is still concerned with us. "

"Why wouldn't the young guy in the Taurus report his conversation with you?"

"The kid doesn't want to end the tail."

"Why would that be?" Portia asked.

Helen tossed her unfinished sandwich in the trash.

"Why don't we just go out there and ask him? Helen said.

Chapter 24

Out in the parking lot, Don climbed into the passenger seat of the Crown Vic, and Helen took a seat in the back. "You should lock your passenger doors. No telling who might want to join you in your car," said Don to the rookie.

"What's your name, son?"

"Sean."

Don's eyes locked onto Sean's face. "You're Pat's son, aren't you?"

"Yes sir."

"Who's Pat?" Helen said.

"Pat Doherty was my partner on the force about ten years ago. Now I know why your face was familiar. Who's your supervisor?"

"Cassidy."

"I'm so sorry."

"Thank you, but I can handle it."

"Why are you tailing me?"

"He told me to."

"What did he say after you told him of our first conversation."

"I didn't tell him."

"Wouldn't that be important?"

"Normally."

"How come you're not following his directions?" Helen asked.

"My dad was Mr. Milkey's partner in KC for seven years," Sean said. "Dad was shot in a holdup at a convenience store in the ghetto. The gunman shot and killed a high school girl who was working the cash register."

"Is your dad still on the force?" Helen asked.

"He died that day."

Helen looked at Don in the front seat. Milkey was looking out the passenger window.

"The police report showed the gunman was shot twice. Once in the leg, and once in the back of the head. The forensics report showed the bullet in the robber's head came from an unregistered handgun, not a police revolver. Before he died, dad said it was his gun. That went into the report."

Don's gaze out the window changed to staring at the dashboard.

"Mr. Milkey changed the police report to reflect that dad shot the gunman in the leg, and Don shot him in the head."

"Don..." Helen started, but didn't finish.

Staring straight ahead, Don said: "my record was already dinged up anyway. I was on my way out."

"That's why Cassidy doesn't get my full report, ma'am. If he takes me off the case, I don't get to learn from a good policeman."

Chapter 25

Milkey sat at the kitchen table in his apartment. He pulled his checkbook closer to him. He removed a rubber band from a stack of envelopes about three inches thick. One by one, he looked inside, and selected two from the pile. He wrapped the rubber band back around the large stack. Don wrote two checks and prepared two envelopes for mailing. He heard movement outside his door and put the checkbook and bills into the drawer in the kitchen.

"Captain Milkey."

Someone knocked hard on the door.

"Captain Milkey. It's me, Garcia."

Don opened the door.

"Hello, Captain, I file my report."

"Garcia, come on in. Want some coffee?"

"No thank you, sir. This is business."

"What do you have?"

"It's report on white van."

"You've seen it again?"

"More than that, Captain."

"Uh...Garcia, call me Don. I've never been a captain, only a lieutenant for a little while."

"Okay, Lieutenant, I got information on the van. It has Maryland license plate, no city decal. It's a new van, and the tires have very few miles. The small guy is about thirty and is a marine."

"What? You saw the occupants?"

"Yes."

"They came out of the van?"

"Yes, one of them."

"They're undercover. Undercover don't show themselves."

"Yes they do, if their van has flat tire."

"You slit their tire?"

" I do not slit tire. I remove valve stem and then replace it when tire is flat."

"Garcia, be careful. You don't know these guys."

"What they going to do, Chief, call cop on me?"

"How do you know one of them is a marine?"

"His tattoo on his arm say: Semper Fidelus. That's Spanish for 'always faithful.'"

"That's Latin, Garcia. And there was someone else in the van?"

"Yes, when back door open, I see big man, a white man. He not smiling."

"So the marine changed the tire."

"No, he pumped it back up."

"He had a tire pump?"

"Yes, I loan him mine."

"You went and got a tire pump?"

"No, I had it with me when tire go flat. I wanted to talk with him."

"What'd he say?"

"Not much. I asked him who he was watching. He said just someone who owed some bills. Like credit card bills I asked him. He say yes. I ask him where he was from. He said Cleveland, but he really from Texas because that's how he talks."

"The other guy?"

"He is big man. I don't mean fat. He is tall and his chest is real big. He look like football player."

"You've done a fine job, Garcia."

"I am good dick?"

"No, you are a good investigator."

"I should not use 'dick'?"

"No."

"The guy in the apartment next to you is Dick. I should not call him by his name?"

"Garcia, you know what I mean."

Garcia smiled. He stood up from the table and walked toward the door. Milkey did likewise.

"We good partners, hey El Capitan?"

"I'm not a captain."

"'El Capitan, that Spanish for 'lieutenant'."

"No it isn't, Garcia. You need to brush up on your Spanish."

"Okay, I call you Don."

"Thanks, Garcia."

"No problem, Chief."

Chapter 26

The hearse stood ready at the front of the funeral home.

"You don't need me," Helen said.

Don looked in the rearview mirror tilted down to reflect his tie.

"How's it look?" Don asked.

"Where's the one I got you?"

"It's at home in the closet. I hate change."

"You call a new tie 'change'?"

"I love this old tie."

"It looks fine. I'll stay in the car. You going to be long?"

"Nah, hand me the photo from the glove compartment."

Helen handed him the photo with Billingsley and Butler in it. Milkey got out of his car and walked into the funeral home.

"Billingsley?" the greeter asked.

"Yes."

"To the left, and then another left."

"Thank you."

Milkey walked down the hall and turned left. There was a small chapel with about twenty people inside. He walked up to the guestbook and wrote his name without any contact information. The signature above his was "Sarah Klein." When he walked into the chapel, he saw her.

"Hello, Mr. Milkey, I thought you might be here," Sarah said.

"No harm in paying respects. You sent the photo to the *Star*?"

Don pulled Sarah toward the back corner of the chapel, away from the other visitors.

"Yes. I felt so bad about Chief Friend. I thought there was something funny going on. I didn't know the details, and I don't care about the details. So, I sent out the photos so someone could finish the job. And the *Star* did."

"You don't feel responsible for his suicide, do you?"

"Oh, hell no. John Friend taught me that we all do things for the force, not for our friends or ourselves. I knew Billingsley was associated with the Klan. I knew this was not good. I saw a number of those guys in the photo come into his office after John died. One was Butler, who I researched and discovered he was a Klan leader in south Missouri. When I found that out, I sent you and the *Star* the photo. I thought you guys would follow up, and I thought the *Star* would write the story about Billingsley. I didn't know Bob would kill himself. But, that's on him. Justice was done in my opinion."

"What do you know about Friend's death?"

"Billingsley moved quickly into John's office, but I don't think Bob was involved. Billingsley may have been doing things to tarnish John's record, but I don't think there was a plan to kill him. He wasn't that evil, and he wasn't good at direct action. What do you think?"

"Well, I'm at a stone wall. I've got few clues."

"I'll do anything to help."

"I may be asking for too much, but it would help us a lot if you knew Friend's username and password for the violations database."

"I'll do anything to help you, Mr. Milkey, but I can't help you with that."

"I understand."

"You take care now," said Don, reaching his hand out. Sarah ignored his hand and embraced him.

"I know you'll work hard on John's case. And then she added: "I know Portia Friend appreciates you, and her cat, Pong, does too."

Chapter 27

Cassidy sat with four patrolmen at a table in the cafeteria at the station. Milkey walked up to the group, looked at Cassidy and smiled.

"Milkey, where you been all these years?" Cassidy said, standing up and reaching out for Don's hand.

"Just doing a little private work," Don said.

"Hey guys, this is Don Milkey. He was with the force until he retired. We need to catch up. Can you guys meet me in my office in about fifteen minutes?"

The four patrolmen got up and left as Cassidy invited Milkey to sit down.

He leaned closer to Don and said, "you son of a bitch, what the hell are you doing in my house? I thought I told you I never wanted to see you again." Spit flew from Cassidy's mouth, barely missing Don.

"Nice to see you again, Chief. Oh, I'm sorry, you're not the chief. I suppose that's just a matter of time."

"What the fuck is it to you? You've got sixty seconds to explain why you and I are having this conversation."

"Sure, Captain. I'll do that. I'll start with a question. Do you have a white van following me?"

"I do not."

"What's your interest in the murder of John Friend?"

"Friend? Who's that?"

"The police chief of Kearney, Missouri."

"Not familiar with the gentleman."

Don stared at Cassidy. "He didn't work for you?"

"The black guy?"

"Yes."

"I remember him, sure. He's dead?"

"Yep. I thought you'd know."

"Nope. Can't keep track of everyone I've worked with. Anything else, Milkey? I've got work to do. Are you familiar with that?"

"I am. One more thing, Captain, and I'll leave. I was hired by Portia Friend to find out who killed her husband. I promised her I would."

"Good luck on that, Milkey," said Cassidy as he stood up. "Are we finished?"

"Yes, but I'll leave you with this: if you have something on this case, and you don't share it with me, you're not going to like the outcome."

"What are you going to do, go to the papers? Ha! You don't want to be in the papers, Milkey, you really don't."

Don looked around the cafeteria.

"Cassidy, you've got a nice place here. You probably have a big office and people who look up to you. Maybe the corner office is in your sights. On the other hand, I boil water for my coffee on my old Westinghouse gas range in my $320 per month apartment in a building I share with people who sometimes get arrested by your department."

"And your point?"

"In a newspaper article, you have more to lose than I do."

"Listen, you little cop wannabe, you come in here accusing me of thinking you're something special that you need a tail, and you think I know about some murder case in a hick town near Kansas City, and you say you're gonna find the person who shot him? Well, good fuckin' luck to you. Go back to your security job."

Cassidy walked away, as Milkey said, "I didn't tell you he was shot, Chief."

Chapter 28

Half the tables in the North Kansas City Starbucks coffee shop had computers open and coffee cups at the ready. He checked to see if anyone had a good view of his screen. No one did, but some of them would be able to see that he had no coffee.

Don scanned the items on the desktop of his new laptop. He clicked on the Word document titled "History Lesson." There was only one word present. It was an internet address link with the word 'kansas' embedded in it. He clicked the link and a login screen popped up. Don typed "Portia", password "Friend." Incorrect. Lower case "portia" and "friend." Incorrect. "portiafriend" and "pong." There was a pause. A search screen came up asking for a plate number. There were blank fields for driver's license number, social security number, phone number, and first and last name.

"John Friend" produced seven Friends and their cities and states. Don chose 'Excelsior Springs, Missouri'.

The screen displayed 18 records. There were parking tickets, a warrant for auto theft, and armed robbery with a notation of armed and dangerous. Except for the first parking ticket, the 'source' field for each of the records was blank. The first parking ticket was put in the system by StLPD. Don picked up his cell phone.

"Jake?"

"Hi, Uncle Don."

"I'm not keeping you from your homework am I?"

"Nope."

"I've got a technical question. I'm into the database, and all I've found is what I already know. Records with no idea who added them."

"You need to sign in as an administrator."

"How do I do that?"

"Click on the button that has 'Admin' on it."

"Got it. There's a new login screen."

"You'll need the username and password for the administrator."

"How do I get that?"

"Use a program on the flash drive, or I can tell you what they are."

"You've got it? Listen Jake, you're providing me tools, not information. I thought we agreed."

"Sure, Uncle Don. Then just crank up the program on the flash drive."

"Okay, give me just the username."

"JayhawkFred, one word, both names capitalized."

"What's the name of the program to find the password?"

"Biology Lesson."

Don clicked on the flash drive. He scanned the file names. He went back to the desktop. He lowered his voice. "Okay, give me the password."

"Write this down, Uncle Don. Remember, these cell phones aren't secure. The third letter of my mom's first name. The second letter of the street we live on. The number of the floor of your apartment. The number of letters in your girl friend's last name. The number of working windows in your car. Got it?"

"Yup. What am I looking for?"

"You're on your own. Snoop around and try things. I'd look for a transaction log. It'd show what records were added or changed and who did the update."

"Jake, I don't know who I'm dealing with on this case. Your mother worries about you. This is good information you've given me, but if someone tracks something back to you, then you could be in danger..."

"Uncle Don,..."

"...and I can't let that happen."

"Uncle Don, I know. I'll be careful. But, you know, I can spend two hours studying history to get another 5% on my test score. Or, I can spend two hours getting information that'll help Portia Friend know what happened to her husband. Did you want me to work on my test?"

Don paused.

Chapter 29

The serving lines at McDonalds had no customers at 8:00 pm. There were four people eating, including Don and Helen.

"Don, I'm concerned about Jeanne and Jake."

"You think they're in danger?"

"I think it won't be long before that white van is parked outside their house."

"How'd you know about the van?"

"Garcia told me when I picked you up tonight."

"Ahh, that Garcia. He's too friendly."

"I'm glad he told me. Now I know why it was parked in the faculty parking lot at Central."

"Really? When?"

"This afternoon when I left school. Billingsley's dead, and someone's still following us."

"I know. I talked to Cassidy today. He said he didn't know the case and then proceeded to show his knowledge of it."

Helen moved her hand closer to Don's.

"Honey, this is getting more complicated and dangerous. I know you and Jake like the same things. But remember, he's just seventeen. And Jeanne doesn't need extra worry. It's tough enough being a single parent."

Don stirred more creamer into his coffee. He watched the swirls until they stopped.

"Helen, I see both sides. Jake's good. He's real good with technology. He's helped me immensely, and I don't know anyone else who I can trust."

" I know you made a promise to Portia, but I think your allegiance here is to your sister and nephew. I'm not sure I want to help you in this case if you can't protect them."

Don stared at his coffee cup.

"I know, I know," he said.

Helen leaned forward. "I couldn't hear you."

"I said I know. I better get going, now. You've got classes early tomorrow, too.

Milkey tapped the button on the answering machine.

"Hey, Don. This is Frank. Just wanted to touch base with you. I haven't seen you for the last five meetings. Call me anytime. I'm here."

Don opened the refrigerator door. At the back of the bottom shelf was an aluminum can. He looked closer. It was diet Coke, not a beer. He held the door open while he gazed at the near empty refrigerator. He scanned all of the shelves again and then closed the door.

He started the six block walk to the ghetto convenience store. A helicopter with a spotlight accompanied him, and the sound of sirens in the distance played tenor to the thuck-a-thuck-a-thuck-a of the roaming chopper.

"Hey, Milkey, what you doing out so late," Jackson said.

"Just picking up a few of your overpriced groceries."

"You need some coupons."

"You give out coupons?"

"No."

Don went over to the refrigerated section at the back of the little store. He lifted out a six-pack of Coors bottles. He picked up a large bag of potato chips on his way to the cash register.

"That gonna be it, Cap'm?"

"That's about all I can afford in this store."

Jackson tallied the purchases on the register.

"That'll be two hundred thirty-seven."

"Ha!" Don said. "Two dollars, thirty-seven."

Jackson reached over to the cigarette section to adjust some of the packages.

"No, Cap'm, that be two hundred thirty-seven dollars." His attention was still on the cigarettes.

"You're serious."

"Yes, sir."

"You're not wanting to sell this to me."

"No, sir. That six-pack's been in the frig for about a year. That's the last time you bought the beer. I brought in about six, seven cases a month just for you, ain't no one else in the neighborhood drinks Coors. That there's my monument for you quittin'. Now you wantin' to destroy my statue. That'll cost ya."

Don took the six-pack and placed it back in the refrigerator. He turned and went to the door.

"Want your chips?"

"Nah."

As Don opened the door, Jackson said, "Cap'm."

Don glanced over at the proprietor.

"You my PI, ain't you?"

Don nodded his head slightly.

"I got your back."

Don glanced in his direction, then down to the floor, he nodded again.

Then he left.

Chapter 30

Jake handed the potatoes to his mother. Meat loaf, string beans, and mashed potatoes occupied the dinner table at Don's sister's house.

"I'm glad you could come over, Portia," Jeanne said. "Don has talked about you so much and told me about your husband."

"Thank you for inviting me. Don told me your husband was a police officer and that you lost him, too," Portia said.

"Yes. Five years ago he was killed by a drug dealer. I know what you're going through," Jeanne said.

"Pass those mashed potatoes. They look good," Portia said.

"Here you go. How'd you meet your husband, if you don't mind talking about it?" said Jeanne.

"He was originally from Monroe, Louisiana. I'm from Kansas City. He was being raised by his grandma down there, along with his two older brothers. Well, those brothers got into some trouble with the law, and each one got involved in a shoot-out with the police. They both died. When John got a little older and more troublesome, his aunt here in Kansas City took him in. I met him at UMKC. His aunt really influenced him."

"Sounds like it," said Jeanne.

"We lived together nearly four years. One day he came home and said he was going to the police academy. I was surprised, but he insisted that's what he wanted."

"How'd you feel about that?" asked Helen.

"In the beginning, I was excited for him. When he made the force, he was so proud. He'd come home and say 'Good guys 1, bad guys 0.' He was on a mission to stamp out evil. He started coming home later, and then he was moved to the night shift, and I began to imagine what might happen to him out on the streets. He assured me he was well trained to watch out for himself, but that wasn't enough. If he was a minute late, I was terror-stricken. The subject of marriage came up, and I told him I couldn't live with fear all my life. I just couldn't be the wife of a patrolman. So he got a desk job for less pay. We got married."

"Well he must have gone back to the street," Don said. "You can't become a chief riding a desk."

"That's right," Portia said. One day he came home from work and when I said 'hi' to him, I said 'Good guys 1?' and he smiled and said, 'Bad guys 0'. We talked about the day's events over supper as we usually did. But that night, it was different. I watched him as he ate and talked. He was smiling, and he told me how good the food was, and he wanted to know every detail of my day. I thought about his older brothers, and I wondered how they could be so different from him. John had every reason to be on the opposite side of the law, but there he was, sitting on the other side of the table, a policeman. He must have seen a greater purpose in his life, and I doubted it was to marry me. So, I told him it was time for him to get his street job back. He grabbed my hand, and told me not to worry; he'd be careful."

There were no tears in Portia's eyes, but they were not dry. " Oh, I've gone on way too long."

"No, thank you for talking about your husband. He had a mission in his life, that's obvious."

"Jake, what's going to be your mission in life?" Portia said.

Jeanne moved her string beans away from her mashed potatoes, then over to the meatloaf.

"Well, I've been thinking about biochemistry." Jake said.

"He's young," said Jeanne. "He may surprise us with a career choice. He's got time. Jake's been doing some research work for Don. He's good at that."

"Pass the meatloaf, Jake," Helen said.

Chapter 31

Brent Iverson entered the elevator and slipped a card into a slot. When he felt the click, he pressed the button for the 8th floor of the Jefferson Building in downtown Denver. At the eighth floor, the door opened, revealing a small reception area with a desk and a chair. An array of monitors hung from the walls. The man sitting at the desk greeted him.

"Good morning, Mr. Iverson, good to see you. Looks like we'll avoid the snow today," the guard said.

"They'll get it in the mountains, for sure," Brent said.

The guard pushed a notebook and pen over to Iverson. Brent signed it and handed the guard his photo ID. The guard looked closely at the picture.

"Is Hopkins here?"

"Yes sir, he's in the conference room."

The guard handed the ID back, and Brent went over to the sign-in pad. The guard pushed a button and the pad lit up. Iverson pushed some keys. The door buzzed and he went in. Across from the entrance was the conference room, where he saw Hopkins. He entered the room and closed the door.

"Did you find Rathbone?" Hopkins asked.

"No."

"I didn't think so. But that's my job, anyway, Brent."

"What have you found out?"

"The investigation of Friend's case has quieted down. The new chief of police killed himself after it became public that he had dealings with a Robert Butler, a Klan leader from Springfield, Missouri. Friend's wife is still pushing, and her PI, Don Milkey, is still involved. He's a private investigator, fired from KCPD, and has been working as a security guard. He's got a Mexican named Garcia working for him. We're keeping an eye on Garcia, and on Milkey's girlfriend. Someone is helping Milkey with technology, and when we find out who, we'll plug into that person, too."

"How about Cassidy?"

"He's handling Friend's murder case. Don't worry about him."

"And Rathbone?"

"He's gone without a trace. We've got no leads. He headed east out of Denver. We've been monitoring his family in Lawrence, and we've got nothing."

"Hopkins, I'm getting nervous."

"Brent, I'm going to turn up the heat on this Milkey guy, maybe even on his girlfriend. Right now, the only threat is Milkey. He's a loose cannon, and Cassidy isn't the brightest. They've got some history between them, and we can't afford to have their conflict reach the papers."

"Do what it takes," said Brent. "And while you're at it, Hopkins, find Rathbone."

"Don't worry. My guys are professionals."

Chapter 32

Don pulled the dust-covered briefcase from the closet in his apartment and placed it on the kitchen table. He took an electronic instrument from the briefcase and placed it on the kitchen counter. As he was cleaning the dust from the case, the needle on the electronic device moved.

Don picked up the briefcase and walked down to his car. The white van was parked across the street . He put the briefcase into the trunk and drove away. Ten minutes later he came back, locked his car, and went back into his apartment. His cell phone rang.

"Honey?"

"Hi Helen."

"Just wanted to bring you up to date on our friends in the white van."

"Great."

"I saw them briefly in the teacher parking lot today. I didn't see anyone come out of the van, but I had a curious letter in my mail box. It was a school form that asked me for my home address and phone number, and name of someone to call in an emergency."

"I don't see how that could be suspicious. You'd be turning that information into someone at school."

"That's the problem. I'm to mail it to the human resources district offices at a P.O. box in Kansas City."

"Save the envelope. We'll check it out."

"You mean go to the Post Office and find out who owns the box." Helen said.

"I'm not sure they will tell you."

"I'll get it out of them."

"Don't make a scene."

"Don't worry, Don. I won't embarrass myself."

"You don't remember that time you threatened that young bank teller?"

"So, that didn't work."

"You still owe me the $100 for the bail."

"Don't you remember, Don? We had sex right after that. That made us even."

"Oh, I forgot. So you only owe me $90."

Chapter 33

The young lady climbed the steps to the third floor of Don's apartment building. She stopped at apartment 301 and knocked on the door.

"Mr. Milkey." She listened for a response. "Mr. Milkey, this is Sandra Schmidt. I'm a reporter for the *Star*. Can you talk?"

Milkey pulled the lever that moved him up and out of his recliner.

"I'm coming."

Don released the dead bolt and the slide bolt and opened the door.

"Hello, Mr. Milkey, I'm Sandra Schmidt. I'd like to talk to you."

Milkey invited her in and offered her a seat at the kitchen table.

"Care for a coffee or tea?" asked Milkey.

"Thank you, tea would be fine."

Don went to the cupboard.

"I'm sorry, I'm fresh out."

"That's okay. If you'd just answer a few questions, that'd be great."

"Did you write the story on Billingsley?" Don asked.

"Yes, I did, with Josh White. He was the one with me at the station when you were there."

"Uh-huh."

"Mr. Milkey, what was your business with Billingsley?"

"I'm a private investigator doing work for a client."

"Who is the client?"

"I'm not at liberty to say."

"Protecting your sources?"

"Yes."

"But you were there to talk to Billingsley."

"Yup."

"Did you know that Billingsley was involved in the Klan?" Sandra asked.

"Yes."

"How did you know?"

"I can't tell you. I have sources, too."

"Do you know a guy by the name of Hunter?"

"I know his name."

"Mr. Milkey, I don't know what you know, but could you just help us? I know you're working for Portia Friend. We reported John Friend's death, but we aren't able to do a follow up. We aren't getting anywhere. Are you?"

"No."

"Would you tell us if you were?"

"Probably not. I work for Portia Friend."

Sandra put her notebook and pen into her briefcase. She spread her hands on the table in front of her.

"Mr. Milkey, I'm not a police officer, or a private investigator. I'm a journalist. I'd like to find out who killed John Friend, just as you would. You're doing it for pay; we're doing it so our readers know what happened. That's our motivation. If you know something, please tell me. If I know something, I'll tell you."

"Miss Schmidt. I'm going to find out who killed John Friend because I told Portia Friend that I would. Look around you; look around this apartment. Surely you don't think I do much for money. Did you interview Hunter?"

" Yes, we did."

"What did you learn from him?"

"That he was just a friend, and proud of him rising to the top of a police force."

"Did you ask Hunter about his own involvement in the death of John Friend?"

"We're a bit more circumspect than you, Mr. Milkey. Hunter did not express much, if anything about John Friend, his death, or his position as police chief."

"You didn't ask him if he had anything to do with Friend's death."

"No, Mr. Milkey, I did not."

"They didn't teach you the direct approach in journalism school."

"They taught us about getting information and not tipping off your interviewee."

"I learned it differently. Asking someone if they killed someone and then watching them real close *is* getting information. You'd be surprised how they start talking or not. That tells you a lot. Not tipping someone off might be good in poker, but in police work, the pot is bigger. It needs stronger action."

"Well, Mr. Milkey, you're a pile of advice for how I should investigate and report."

Sandra picked up her briefcase, stood up from the table.

"Thanks for your time, Mr. Milkey."

"You're welcome Ms. Schmidt. I'll walk you down to your car."

Milkey waved to Sandra as her car pulled onto the street.

Don opened his car trunk. There was a spare tire, but nothing else.

Chapter 34

...you get in trouble with the man...

"Hello, Portia?"

"Have you received a call from Sarah Klein, Billingsley's receptionist?"

"Nope."

"I just did, and you're not going to believe this. She learned through some Kearney patrolmen, that the Missouri highway patrol pulled over the police chief of Birmingham, Missouri last night."

"For sixteen parking tickets?"

"No, just ten."

"They didn't shoot him."

"No, they didn't."

"Don't tell me...he's black?"

"Oh, no, Mr. Milkey, he's not black. I'm surprised you jumped to that conclusion."

"Latino?"

"Yes."

"Kearney Police Department, this is Sarah Klein, how may I help you?"

"Sarah, this is Don Milkey."

"Ah, Portia called you. I thought she would."

"What's the guy's name?"

"I've looked it up, it's Henry Gonzales."

"You don't know him?"

"I recognize the name, but that's all."

"Did Billingsley know him?"

"I don't think so, but I don't know for sure."

"Did John Friend know him?"

"John knew a lot of people. It's likely he would have met a number of police chiefs, especially if one was Latino. But I don't recall any communication with Gonzales."

Milkey entered a small Butler Building in Birmingham.

"Mr. Gonzales, a Mr. Milkey is here to see you."

"Who is he?"

"He says he's a private investigator representing a Mrs. Friend."

"Would you ask him to set up an appointment for tomorrow afternoon?" The secretary left and then came back.

"He says he's sorry to intrude, but he represents the wife of John Friend, the Kearney police chief who was killed. He also added he wanted to ask about your parking tickets."

"Send him in."

"How well did you know John Friend, Mr. Gonazles?"

"I'd say he was an acquaintance. Our paths crossed about once a year."

"How many traffic tickets did you have?"

"You mean legitimate ones?"

"Those and the others."

"I had one, and the rest of the record is fully false."

"Which was legitimate?"

"My first parking ticket."

"Where did you get it?"

"Downtown St. Louis, at the annual Security Convention."

Chapter 35

The receiver/recorder on Don's kitchen table came alive.

"What's our schedule?"

"We're here at Milkey's for four hours this morning, and then on to Rathbone ."

"I'm wondering why we're here when all we're getting from the bug are some gushing sounds."

"We're not paid to wonder."

"Where'll we be looking for Rathbone?"

"The downtown library and then some branches. Tech isn't seeing any traffic from him on the internet. That means he's not on his own computer, or visiting any of his usual sites. He's not even been to his two bank accounts."

"They think he's using some public computers. I guess it's worth a chance. But, what he's doing for money? He's got to eat."

"Someone's helping him with computer access and room and board."

"No doubt. Shhh!"

"What do you hear?"

"It sounds like water running."

"Joe, I think he's got something interfering with the bug. I hear some words in the background."

"Can you make them out?"

"Let's play it back."

"Do you hear it?"

"I think so."

"What's he saying? In the background"

"He's saying '...Miss Rosie...umbrella on her shoulder...'."

"Who's Miss Rosie?"

"Beats me."

"We'll just send in the tape; let them figure it out."

Chapter 36

The door to the convenience store opened and a woman walked in carrying a Saks Fifth Avenue bag, its handles reinforced by duct tape. The man following her wore a Chicago Cubs baseball cap with dirt on the bill.

"Kevin, get some pork and beans and some saltines, will ya? I'll get us somethin' to drink."

The woman walked toward Jackson who was behind the cash register and in front of the pint and half-pint liquor bottles.

"Mornin' sir," she said.

"Morning," Jackson said. "Ruby, right?"

"Ruby? Do I look like a 'Ruby'? I'm Lulu. That's 'Lu', twice."

"Lulu, what can I get for you?"

"I'll have a pint of Knob Creek, and...ah...hold it, hey Kevin, what'dya want?"

"I'm good."

"...okay, two pints of Knob Creek," Lulu said.

"You know you could get a fifth for less than two pints."

"Nah, we've got transportation problems, here. A pint size is just right for our pockets."

Kevin walked up to the cashier, carrying three cans of pork and beans, some saltine crackers, and a roll of small chocolate doughnuts.

"Have I missed anything, Lulu?"

"Looks like you got it all. Oh, you got some matches?" she asked Jackson.

"I've got some wooden matches there for about a buck, or some giveaways from my liquor supplier for free. They don't say 'Knob Creek' on them, though."

"Ha!" said Lulu. "We'll take them free ones."

"Need some smokes?" Jackson asked.

"No, I got two day's supply."

"How 'bout your partner?"

"He don't smoke. He's afraid of getting some 'pulminory' thing. That's his word."

Lulu put her own empty bag on the counter. "Here, use mine, I got it broken in."

"You shop at Saks?" Jackson asked.

"Oh, hell no. But I got nothing against using their bags. I got this out of a dumpster downtown. It had a blouse in it about ten sizes too small for me. I use it for a wash rag, though. Hey, a poor gal's gotta use all of the steer, if ya know what I mean.

"I do," Jackson said.

"I'm puttin' in a bag of chips for you. They gone past their expiration date, do you mind?"

"We ain't picky. You got a problem with expiration dates, Kevin?"

"Nope."

The two thanked Jackson and left the store. The proprietor watched as Lulu swung her bag away from the closing door. He caught a glimpse of Kevin's shoes. They were ecco brand walking shoes.

Chapter 37

"Want some tea?" Don asked everyone around his kitchen table.

"You don't have any tea," Helen replied.

"I was just being polite."

"I'll have some coffee," Helen said.

"And you, Garcia?"

"I like some tea," said Garcia.

"I don't have any."

"You find tea behind oatmeal in your cupboard."

"Garcia, you come into my apartment to fix my garbage disposal and you rifle through my cupboards?"

"I don't have gun."

"It's a figure of speech. It means 'rummage' or 'snoop'."

"Or 'investigate'?" Garcia asked.

"Hardly. So you want some tea, now?"

"Coffee okay, boss."

Don poured two cups of coffee.

"We now have two 'victims,' John Friend and Henry Gonzales. Both police chiefs, both attended a convention in St. Louis, both received parking tickets for parking on the street in downtown St. Louis. Both minorities, and both started getting fake charges on their record. Furthermore, I am being tailed by an undercover patrolman under the direction of Captain Cassidy. Also, we are all under watch by two guys in a white van. And, they are searching for a guy by the name of 'Rathbone'."

"What do you want from us?" Helen asked.

"Theories."

"Okay, here's one," Helen said. "There will be more victims, all having attended the Security Convention in St. Louis."

"Next victim will be white," Garcia said.

"What?" Don said. "Don't we see a trend here?"

"How do you say it? Stomach feel?"

"Stomach feel?" Don asked.

"Gut feeling," Helen said.

"Gut feel, yes. I feel it, I don't know it," said Garcia.

"Evidence, Garcia, not gut feel."

"Evidence and gut feel, El Capitan."

"We need to find out who was at the convention." Helen said. "We contact them to ask about their driving records. We don't know when someone becomes a victim. John was killed. Henry was pulled over. The other victims may not have tripped a switch, but are still in danger."

"Great idea. Would you do it?"

"Sure," Helen said.

"Also, we need to know more about Rathbone. I'll do some research on the name."

"And me, Captain?"

"Fix my garbage disposal."

"But, I'm your assistant. I try to be good dick. Now you want something fixed."

"Okay, take this recorder. It records every time the receiver is actuated. Make sure it works that way. I will need to know each time it records."

"Yes, boss. I call you boss?"

"No, call me Don."

"Okay, Chief."

Chapter 38

"Kearney Police."

"Sarah, Don Milkey."

"Oh, thanks for calling back so quick. Listen, I just got a call from Henry Gonzalez at the Birmingham Police Department."

"More charges?"

"No, more people. His brother-in-law in Bolivar, Missouri. Six traffic tickets."

"The first one in St. Louis?"

"No, in Bolivar. But, he was at the convention in St. Louis."

"He's a police chief?"

"No. He's director of security for Stop and Go convenience stores."

"Tell me he's Latino."

"No, he's white. His name is Samual Bolin. He's known as 'Sammy Bo'."

"Thanks for keeping me informed, Sarah."

"You're welcome. And one last thing, Mr. Milkey. I've got relatives in the Springfield area, just south of Bolivar. They've heard about Sammy Bo. He's associated with the Minutemen militia. Has a big Confederate flag decal in the back window of his pickup."

"I didn't need that information, Sarah. Now I have to readjust my theories."

Sara chuckled. "Glad to help."

"Don...Don...pick up the damn phone. It's Helen. Get out of your recliner and go over and pick up your phone..."

"I got it. Hi Helen."

"I knew you were there. Geez, don't you ever answer your phone?"

"No."

"Well you would've missed out on some interesting information."

"You got information on the St. Louis convention?"

"Yup. Isn't that what you wanted? I've got the whole list of attendees, four thousand, thirty-seven of them."

"Great!

"I've got names, titles, addresses, phone numbers, affiliations."

"Ages, race?"

"No and no."

"Where are they from?"

"The midwest area, Missouri, Illinois, Iowa, Arkansas, Minnesota."

"Are they mostly police chiefs?"

"No. They are mostly from law enforcement, but there are people in security positions, too. Corporate guys. Security Guard companies."

"Who had the list?"

"The event planner, named 'Convention Conveners'. They're a Chicago firm."

"And they just gave you the list?"

"Oh, silly you, I had to buy the thing. It was for sale. A thousand dollars."

"Where'd you get the thousand?"

"Don, you know me. I don't pay retail. It cost me three hundred and a promise to them that they could do our security guard convention in Oklahoma City."

"You told them we're doing a convention in Oklahoma City?"

"No I didn't. I allowed them to infer that."

"That's lying."

"I call that, 'allowing someone to infer something'."

"Without correcting them."

"Hey, they were busy, and I was out of time. We just didn't cover all the facts."

"I'm stunned by your lack of honesty."

"No you aren't, Don. I learned this from you. You call it, 'telling the truth in due time'."

"Oh, yeah. That's right."

"I'm not calling this list," said Helen.

"Why not?"

"I don't have the time."

"You don't have a few hours?"

"Four thousand times five minutes a call equals 20,000 minutes divided by 60 = about 333 hours. I love you a lot, but not that much."

"I'll do it."

"Now, Don, don't do that passive-aggressive thing on me, please."

"No, I'll do it, no problem, no regrets."

"Okay, I'll call half the list."

"No, that's not necessary. Don't worry about it."

"Maybe Garcia can take a third of it."

"You mean have the guy whose English is his third language talk to people on the phone?"

"Third?"

"At least. Okay, Helen, I confess, I can do the list one minute per person."

"How."

"I'll tell you later."

"Is it a secret?"

"No, it's 'truth in due time'."

"I understand, you lying asshole."

"I love it when you talk that way."

"Anything on the guy Rathbone?"

"I googled him, got about three million hits."

"You need a first name."

"I tried his name in Kansas City, St. Louis, and Kearney, but I don't know what I'm looking for on those hits. Is he on the convention list?"

"No, I looked. There's a Rathburne in Columbia, Missouri, who is a security guard, but I wasn't sure what I'd ask him if I got him on the phone."

"Well, if the guys in the van are correct, this guy has made himself small. That would happen if Rathbone feared these people, and feared for his life. That would put him in the same category as Friend, Gonzalez, and Bolin."

"Not quite, Don. Those three guys, at least the first two did not see anything coming. I think that puts Rathbone in a position to threaten the white van."

"Or whoever has hired the white van."

"We not only have to find out who Rathbone is, but who it is that is interested in finding him too."

"Of course this only makes sense if you and Rathbone are linked."

"By John Friend."

"Right."

"You're pretty smart. Honey, you still there? I meant to say that you're pretty fucking smart, you sumbich."

"Thank you, Helen, I needed that."

Chapter 39

Don pulled into the McDonald's parking lot at Rainbow and 47th. He walked into the restaurant, strode directly past the counter and exited the other side of the building. The black Crown Victoria with the young man inside was parked in a lot adjacent to the restaurant.

"Hello, Sean," said Milkey, as he sat down in the passenger seat.

"Mr. Milkey, how ya doing?"

"I've got some questions for you, but I need to know first that our meeting here won't get back to Cassidy."

"Don't worry."

"Is there an investigation of John Friend's death going on in the department?"

"I haven't heard of one, but I'm not that well informed."

"What's Cassidy's interest in me?"

"He doesn't like you."

"Has he told you why you're tailing me?"

"I asked him. He said I didn't need to know."

"Is anyone else tailing me?"

"With Kansas City?"

"Yes."

"No. But you've got a white van parked outside your apartment complex."

"How do you know they're interested in me?"

"It's an expensive vehicle with out of town plates. They're not interested in minor players in your apartment. That narrows it down to you."

"Sean, I realize I'm putting you out on a limb here. Just tell me when to stop, and I will. I can't run plates. Could you do something to help me on this without Cassidy knowing? I'd understand if you couldn't. "

"Mr. Milkey, I want to help you, but I'm a rookie. Rookies follow rules to advance their careers. It's a risk me just sitting here in this car with you. I'm okay with not telling Cassidy about our conversations, but I can't help you conduct an investigation. Me and my family owe you big time, but I can't pay you back that way."

"You're just like your father, Sean. I can't ask you to act any differently. I'm grateful for the risk you've already taken for me."

"Thank you, Mr. Milkey."

"I see you've gotten rid of your hats. That's good. But this black Crown Vic with the blackwalls has 'Cop' written all over it. The blue Taurus was better."

"You're right. That blue car was much better, but, unfortunately, it was involved in an accident, and it's in the shop getting its back bumper repaired. You might know about that little incident."

"Can't say that I do, Sean. You young guys are always running into things."

Chapter 40

"Jake, I've got a technical question."

"Go ahead."

"I've got a file of about four thousand names and addresses. I want to run it against the national database to see if any names appear."

"What format is the file in?"

"Spreadsheet."

"What're you looking for?" Jake asked.

"Convention attendees who have lots of parking tickets."

"No problem. In fact, I did some research on my own. I've got a file of records from the national database that have no sources."

"What?"

"I just wrote a program that sought out blanks in the source field."

"Is there a Henry Gonzales and Samuel Bolin on the list?"

Jake did not respond.

"Jake?"

"Yeh."

"Did you hear me?"

"Yeah, I'm looking for them."

"Well, how many records are there?"

"About five hundred."

"Five hundred people with no sources on their violations?"

"No, five hundred violations, not five hundred people. It looks like each person has about eight or nine records. That would be about fifty or sixty people. And Bolin and Gonzalez are there, with Friend."

"I need that file. Can I come over and get it?"

"I'll email it to you. The file will be encrypted. There is a program on the flash drive I sent you that can open the file."

"What do the records contain?"

"Date of entry, first and last name, driver's license, plate number, violation, and source, which is blank, of course."

"No address?"

"Not in this file, but I think it's available."

"It would be helpful if you could dump the whole record."

"I'll do it. You'll get the first file immediately. I'll send the second one as soon as I can."

"This number I'm calling you at, is it your Mom's land line?"

"No, it's my Skype number."

"Is it traceable?"

"No, not likely. It's a new one and only you and I use it. Also, if you call and I don't answer, don't leave a message. Just hang up. I turn off Skype when I'm not using it. When I turn it back on, I'll see you called. I'm just trying to stay off the net as much as possible. And when you open my email attachment, save it to the flash drive. Then shut down your internet connection. You need to keep a low profile, too."

"Jake, you're doing great work here."

"Thanks."

"I promised your mom I wouldn't take you away from your other school subjects."

"I know. We talked. She's worried more about my being involved in your murder case. She said she'd feel better if I told her everything I was doing."

"Your dad married a smart woman. Do what she says."

"I will."

Chapter 41

"Where you from, Kevin?" asked Lulu as they walked back from the store.

"I'm from west of here," said Kevin.

"Well that kinda cuts it in half, don't it?"

"What's your concern? You don't know where anyone else is from either."

"Oh, you think I don't."

"What, are you some kind of detective, Lulu?"

"You might say that. Take Bikerman. He's from Duluth."

"He told you?"

"In one way or another. One day I asked him if he wanted to go to the Laundromat with me, he said he didn't have anything to wash. But he didn't say 'wash', he said 'warsh'. That's how they say it up north."

"How'd you get it narrowed down?"

"Well, ya gotta have patience. You wait for other clues. I asked him one day if he'd ever been to Williston. He was puzzled. He didn't know North Dakota. That moved it on east."

"What about me?"

"You're from Lawrence, Kansas," said Lulu, looking closely at Kevin's face.

"What makes you think that?"

"You been to college. Lawrence is west of here. It could be Boulder, too."

"You read a lot of mystery novels?"

"Hell, Kevin, I been in a lot of mysteries. It's Boulder, isn't it? If it was Lawrence, you wouldn't have said 'west of here.' That would have been too close. Boulder's the one. Now all I have to do is figure out your degree."

"You haven't been a detective earlier in your life, Lulu?"

"Nope, but been on the other end of that stick too many times. You've been a scientist, haven't you, Kevin?"

"What would make you say that?"

"Easy, you're a careful person. You pack up your sleeping bag just right. Others just throw their blankets into a bag. You square yours off. That means you don't teach literature. Also, I know it now, because you didn't show any reaction to me guessing it right."

"You're sure."

"Yep, and I'd say you were a computer scientist."

"How did you know?"

"I didn't. I guessed. And now you've proved it."

"I'm not talking to you anymore," said Kevin.

"Suit yourself, honey. But that won't stop me from finding stuff out about you."

"No doubt. But now I know about you."

"Yeah, sweetie, but you won't get even close to my story."

"Not sure I want to."

"You don't, honey, believe me."

Chapter 42

Don underlined a name and the phone number on the spreadsheet report.

"Hello, is this Franklin Smith?"

"Yes it is."

"Sorry to bother you this morning. I'm Joe Johns, and I'm employed by Chicago Conveners; we put on the security convention in St. Louis last month, and we're taking a survey of the attendees to get your opinions about how things went. Do you have a few minutes?"

"A few minutes, yes."

"What was the purpose of your attending?"

"Well, me and the wife run a little security business in northern Iowa, along with my brother-in-law. That convention was a trip to get up to date on the industry and also hit the casinos a bit."

"Which speaker interested you the most?"

"The guy, I forget his name, the guy from Chicago who talked about the cameras and monitors."

"We brought in some important people in the field. I'm going to ask if you remember talking with them. Their names are: John Friend, Henry Gonzales, and Samuel Bolin. Do you recognize these names?"

"Well I talked to a lot of people, and traded some business cards, but I don't remember those names, specifically. I might have met them and didn't know it."

"How'd you like the downtown setting for the convention?"

"It was great. Loved it."

"Did you have any trouble with parking?"

"Nope."

"You parked in the hotel parking lot?"

"Oh, hell no, we aren't high rollers. We parked on the street."

"How did that work out?"

"We had to be on our toes. We parked at a one-hour parking meter, and either me or my wife dashed down to our car and kept it legal."

"We've had several of the attendees get parking tickets at the convention. Did that happen to you, if I may ask."

"Nope, we didn't get any."

"I want to thank you, Mr. Smith, for your time and opinion. "

"No problem, enjoyed the convention."

"One other thing, Mr. Smith, and it's not part of the survey, and I don't even know if it's a big thing or not, but several convention attendees reported to me that they parked their cars on the streets and were cited for parking violations that they didn't know about. You might want to talk to your local police to see if your record is clean. I don't know how it happened, but these guys didn't know about the parking tickets."

"Thanks for the heads up. I'll check it out. And, before you hang up, will you be having any more security conventions in the Midwest?"

"I believe there will be one in Oklahoma City in a couple of months. We'll be contacting you with upcoming events."

Chapter 43

"Garcia, where are you from?" Milkey asked.

"Apartment 100, boss."

"No, I mean, where do you come from?"

"Pueblo, Colorado."

"You were born in Pueblo?"

"No, boss."

"Where were you born?"

"In a hospital."

"Where was the hospital? What city?"

"I don't know. I was very young."

"Garcia, I want to ask you a question, but I don't know if you can tell me."

"I understand, boss. You want to know if I'm gay."

"No, I don't."

"You no care?"

"Yes, I care. Okay, are you gay?"

"No. Do I act gay, boss?"

"No, you don't. You brought up the subject."

"Garcia, do you know what 'GPS' stands for?

"Garcia Pretty Smart?"

"GPS is global positioning system."

"Ah, I know."

Don reached into a cardboard box under the kitchen table, and pulled out a black box.

"This is a GPS. This big box is the receiver, the little one the transmitter."

"You want me to put this into white van."

"You're going to make a good dick.

"You tell me not to use that word."

"I'm joking with you, Garcia. Like you're doing with me?"

"I no joke. My face is straight all the time."

"How're you going to do this, Garcia, without the people inside knowing about it?"

"I create diversity."

"Huh?"

"A diversity. You know, like you poke someone in eye, and then kick him in nuts when he no see."

"Uh...that works if you're fighting someone. That's called a diversion."

"Diversion, yes. I get one guy to leave van, and then get the other to look what's happening, and then get the GPS under a seat, or somewhere else."

"You can do this?"

"Yes, but not by myself."

"Do you need my help?"

"No, captain, I have friends."

"Do these friends have records?"

"Yes, captain, they do. They like Percy Sledge."

"Percy Sledge was in jail?"

"No, he just sang songs."

Chapter 44

Cecil Khan looked out of the 8th floor conference room window. "Can you see Coors Field from here?"

Brent Iverson put his hand on Cecil's shoulder and guided him to another window. "There it is." Iverson pointed to the home of the Colorado Rockies.

"Beautiful. I love this city. Not as much as San Diego, of course. Are you originally from Denver, Brent?"

"No, born and raised in Chicago."

"A little cold for my warm nature," Cecil said. "Let's get right down to it, Brent. I've got a tee time at 1:00 this afternoon. Tell me the good news about my million dollar investment."

"We've nailed it, Cecil. We've got ten installations around Denver, Cheyenne and one in western Kansas. Panther is working like a charm. When bank presidents understand the concept, and they see the demo, they pull out their checkbooks and ask how much."

Cecil smiled.

"Keep in mind, we've only started with the independent banks. We've got appointments with Bank of America, and with Chase. As we described in our business plan, we're perfecting it on the smaller banks before we hit the chains."

"What's making this work, Brent? What's the secret to our success?"

"It's the algorithm. Panther is a stone wall. No hacker can touch it."

"I'm sure glad you hired Dr. Rathbone. He's the key, right?"

"That's for sure. We're lucky he agreed to head up the project."

"I thought he'd be at this meeting."

"He was going to be here, but something has come up."

"Well get him on the phone. I'd like to talk with him."

Brent picked up his cell phone. "Thornton, would you come in here. Cecil wants to talk to Rathbone. I think you have his private cell number."

The door to the conference room opened, and Thornton Hopkins walked in.

"Cecil."

"Hey, Thornton, got time for golf this afternoon? You too, Brent."

"Nah, I got this little project going on and our investor is all over us to get it done."

"Ha."

"Thornton, you got Rathbone's private cell number?"

"I do, but don't you remember, Brent? Kevin's taking a week to recharge."

"He's taking time off just when the project is setting sail?" Cecil asked.

"He was critical to the design and development work, and that job is ninety-eight percent complete."

"Well dial him up anyway. I want to talk with him."

"I'm afraid that's not possible. He's in Utah somewhere, and I don't think he's got a signal. I tried him early this morning. Sorry."

"I'm disappointed with you boys. I wrote a check for a million dollars and did you the courtesy of being hands off. I come to Denver to get a summary of the project, and I learn the head scientist is off on vacation. I'm going to need some reassurance here."

Hopkins wrote a number on a piece of paper. "Cecil, I tell you what. Here's his number. We'll call it. You call it. And if we can't contact him, we'll track him down and have him call you. Believe me, his work is pure genius, but it's mostly done. If he was struck down by lightning, we would proceed without much of a hitch."

"I don't like how this smells, gentlemen. I've got a tee time, I gotta go. Don't let me down on this. I'll fly into Denver five times a week if need be. You don't want that."

Cecil left the conference room, and the elevator doors shut without him giving a glance back.

Hopkins looked at Iverson. "What an asshole. He thinks Rathbone not being here is a problem."

Iverson chuckled. "Boy, is he in for a big surprise. He's gonna call me one day and he'll hear an electronic voice saying my number is no longer in service. Ha. He'll shit his pants. What number did you give him?"

"I gave him Rathbone's company cell number. No way Khan will get to him. When he gets back to San Diego, I'll have one of the scientists give Cecil a call and pretend to be Rathbone. He won't know the difference."

"But we gotta find Rathbone."

"Yup."

Chapter 45

Don and Helen sat at his kitchen table with the phone book opened to the white pages.

"We're assuming he lives in Kansas City," Helen said.

"And that he has a land line listed in the phone book." Don said.

Don's cell phone rang.

"Hello, Jake, I need to find someone."

"What's their name?"

"I only have his last name. Rathbone. R-a-t-h-b-o-n-e."

"That all?"

"Someone is searching for him, someone interested in John Friend and me."

"Who's searching for him?"

"Don't know."

"How old is he?"

"Don't know."

"This isn't much."

"I know. All I know is what I've learned from the guys who've been staking me out. They believe he is off the grid. No phone, no internet, no banking. They're looking for him in libraries where he could have access to computers."

"Then he's computer literate."

"Hmm, that's right."

Jake paused. "And if he knows the grid, then he's more than computer literate."

"What do you mean?"

"If they can't find him, then he must know the dangers of using his phone, the internet, ATM machines, and his credit or debit cards. He knows what's possible. He's sophisticated."

"You've got a point there, Jake."

"I've got some ideas, Uncle Don. I'll call you."

Don opened the white pages to the 'R's. He moved his finger down the page. "Here, there are six of them."

"I'll start at the top, you start at the bottom," Helen said.

"Hello, Mrs. Rathbone?"

"Yes?"

"This is Frank Lutz with the phone company. We're making some changes to your service to limit telemarketing. Do you have a few minutes to help us?"

"Oh, sure."

"Have you had any telemarketing calls in the past week?"

"No."

"How about your husband or your children?"

"Oh, my children are all grown up, and my husband has been dead for ten years."

"Oh, I'm sorry. Thanks for your help, Mrs. Rathbone."

"Hello, Mr. Rathbone?"

"Yes."

"This is Betty Lutz with Lutz plumbing."

"Yes."

"You called us this morning about a clogged sewer line?"

"Nope. We don't have any problems with that. If we did, we wouldn't be calling you. I'm a plumber myself."

"I must have the wrong number. Sorry to bother you."

"Hello, Mrs. Rathbone?"

"Yes?"

"This is Don Milton down at First State Bank. I wanted to call and offer you and your husband an opportunity to buy a high-rate CD."

"We're not really interested."

"You might be interested in the luncheon we're having down at Carozzo's this Saturday..."

"...Frankly, Mr. Milton, I'm not interested, and my husband is gone."

"Gone?"

"Yup. Haven't seen or heard from him in two weeks."

"I'm sorry to hear that. Have you filed a missing person's report?"

"Hell no. He was screwing his secretary, and I found out about it. I'm glad he's gone, and he could be in Timbuktu, for all I care."

"I'm sorry."

Click.

"Uncle Don, it's Jake."

"What'd you find?

"I've got a few names, but you need to know my logic because there're thousands of Rathbones around."

"Let's hear it."

"I focused on the hacking of the database."

"Okay."

"I put Rathbone in the role of the hacker."

"Why would you think that?"

"No reason. I arbitrarily assigned him."

"All right."

"That makes him one of two types of people. He's either a street geek with an internet connection and a boatload of time and brains, or he's a Ph.D. in some field related to computers."

"Did you arbitrarily assign Rathbone to one of those types?"

"No. Street geeks are in it for the fun and chaos. A Ph.D. has a narrower purpose, like screwing with security conference attendees."

"So you're looking for Ph.D.'s."

"Not just any one. If you've got a higher degree it means you're good at jumping through hoops and coloring inside a department's lines. Geeks don't have that experience. I looked for only the top graduates at the universities known for their technology programs: Carnegie-Mellon, MIT, and Stanford. I found seven graduates with the name of Rathbone, three of them women. The men were Thomas, Franklin, Cornwall, and Kevin. The first two studied artificial intelligence, Cornwall's specialty was programming theory, and Kevin's was database design."

"Do you have where they live and where they work?"

"Yup."

"Email the details on the men."

"Will do."

"Hello, Mrs. Rathbone?"

"Yes."

"May I speak to Dr. Rathbone. This is Lincoln with the university."

"Yes, this is Dr. Rathbone."

"Oh, I'm sorry, I was looking for a Dr. Rassmussen. I'm sorry."

"Hello, Mrs. Rathbone?"

"Yes?"

"This is Dr. Milton with the National Association of Computer Scientists. May I speak to Kevin?"

"Kevin's not here."

"Oh, did he go to our convention in San Antonio?"

" I'm not sure I've heard of your organization."

"Do you expect him home tonight? Would that be a better time to call him?"

"No."

"Uh...Mrs. Rathbone, it's pretty important to contact him. There is some issue with his credentials."

"You mean his dissertation?"

"Well, that's the problem. You see, Carnegie-Mellon doesn't have his dissertation on record."

"I can't believe that."

"I know. It sounds far-fetched, and I'm sure it's just an oversight somewhere. Maybe you could have him call me."

"He's not available to do that."

"Thank you, Mrs. Rathbone, I'll call him at work tomorrow. That's. Transnational Security ..."

"No. it's Innovative Security Solut...who are you now?"

"Dr. Cornelius Lincoln. I'm a fellow member with Kevin in the NACS."

"Kevin never mentioned your organization."

"It's a highly respected group, and most of our members are from Carnegie-Mellon. If I could ask you one more thing..."

"I'm sorry, I'm not really sure who you are."

Click.

"That was him?" Helen asked.

"That's him. Kevin Rathbone, who works for 'Innovative Security Solutions'."

"I'll search the internet for their location."

Chapter 46

A woman wearing a man's overcoat stood at the cashier's cage.

"Half pint of 'Knob Creek'," she said.

Jackson pulled the small bottle off the shelf and wrapped it in a bag.

Lulu counted out four dollars and fifty-seven cents in quarters, dimes, nickels and pennies. "Here you go." She pushed the change toward Jackson.

The door to the convenience store opened and Milkey walked in.

"Hey, Cap'm."

"Jackson."

Lulu looked at Milkey, and hurried past him to the door.

Milkey walked the aisles, picking up bologna and cheese and bread.

"Do you have any mustard?" Don asked.

"On the second aisle, bottom shelf, but don't be lookin' at expiration dates."

"Jackson, this mustard is seven months out of date."

"It's just gettin' good, Cap'm. Try it."

"Alright, I'm trusting. If it's bad, can I get a refund?"

"Yeah. Just bring your receipt in."

"Jackson, I've never gotten a receipt from you in the last five years."

"I guess that explains me never giving a refund."

Don carried his groceries to the cage.

"Jackson, you're an astute man. You can probably help me."

"What'd you call me, an ass what?"

"Astute."

"What's that mean?"

"It means you're knowledgeable."

"Okay. Maybe about some things."

"Tell me this, Jackson, if you didn't want anyone to find you in Kansas City, where'd you go?"

"Chattanooga."

"No, Jackson, I meant if you were staying in Kansas City."

"Well, Cap'm, I'd be in this part of town. Right here. I wouldn't be using a credit card, no phone, no car. Lulu, she'd be an example of someone hiding, but I don't think she is. She's just enjoying a low profile."

"Who's Lulu?"

"The lady who just left."

"Homeless?"

"Yup. Tell me more about the guy you're looking for."

"He's a computer scientist. He's been threatened. He's not in touch with anyone. No one knows where he is."

"I've seen him."

"What?"

"He was in my store with Lulu."

"How do you know he's the guy."

"He was wearing a $150.00 pair of shoes, eccos."

"When was that?"

"About a half pint ago. Two days."

"Where do they hang out?"

"They's under the bridges in the downtown loop. From Broadway to the Paseo. But I wouldn't go lookin' for them; they'll scatter like cockroaches when a light turns on."

Don paid for his groceries. He handed Jackson an additional hundred dollar bill.

"Jackson, next time you see Lulu, get her to bring Kevin to your store, will you?"

"Aw...Cap'm, I don't know if that'll work. These people like their booze and the money to get the booze, but they kinda funny. They don't put theirselves in each other's business. They loners. Don't think a hundred would work."

"Maybe I could talk to Lulu."

"Maybe, maybe not. Did you see her hurry out past you?"

"No."

"She smelled the law."

"What's that smell like, Jackson?"

"I don't know Cap'm, but you never know what's happened to these guys."

"I need to talk to her."

"Alright, next time she's in, I'll call you. You come down and try to talk to her." Jackson bagged Don's groceries, and Milkey left the store. As he opened the door to leave, Jackson said, "Cap'm?"

"Yeah?"

"You my PI ain't you?"

"Yup."

"These street people, they's my customers. You take good care of 'em, won't you?"

"I will, Jackson."

Chapter 47

"Mr. Milkey, this is Jackson down at the store. Your order is available, you can pick it up anytime."

"Lulu?"

"Yes sir, that's right, it just came in. You probably need to park your truck at the side entrance."

"Will do. Thanks, Jackson."

Lulu moved around the store, asking prices on the cans of peas. She gathered a few cans of soup, two cans of beans, and some cookies.

When she reached the cashier, Jackson was still on the phone.

"Yes, honey. Yes, babe. I will. Don't worry. I will."

Lulu waited while Jackson talked.

"I know, I know. Things'll be different from now on. I know what you're saying. You right on this babe. Okay, see you tonight at about 10. Some chips? Sure, I'll bring 'em. Maybe a little wine, hey babe? You too."

"A little woman trouble there?" Lulu asked.

"Oh, you know it. Man looks at another woman, maybe even just her scarf, and that turns into cheating in your woman's mind. Gotta be careful around my lady friend."

"Some women have extramarital perception," Lulu said.

"Thas for sure."

"Give me a half-pint."

"What brand?"

"Knob Creek, don't ya remember me?"

"I sure do, but you may want somethin' else."

The door opened, and Milkey walked in.

"Good evening,...sir."

Lulu looked around to see Don walking over to the chip display.

"How much do I owe you," Lulu asked.

"Well, let see."

Jackson took his time in totaling up the groceries and the half pint. Milkey carried a bag of chips up to the cashier's cage.

"How much?" Lulu asked again.

"$17.47," Jackson said.

"How do you do, ma'am," Milkey said.

"Fine," Lulu said.

"I used to drink Knob Creek, myself."

"Oh?"

"Not all that smooth, but the price was right."

Lulu nodded her head slightly.

"Lulu, this is Mr. Milkey, a good customer of mine."

Lulu did not respond.

"He's looking for someone who's disappeared."

"I ain't talkin' to no cop."

Lulu hurriedly put the half pint in the grocery bag and turned to go.

"I'm not a cop. I'm a private investigator, and I'm looking for someone who killed my client's husband."

"Can't help you."

"I'm looking for a guy who's pretty smart. His name is Rathbone, Kevin Rathbone."

"Don't know anyone who's smart."

The front door opened and two young men came in.

"Lulu, I know Milkey. He's okay. You can trust him. And this Rathbone isn't a suspect, is he, Cap'm?"

"Nope."

"Why don't you guys go back in my office where you can talk while I help my customers."

Chapter 48

Papers and files littered the surface tops in Jackson's office. There were four chairs and a desk. Some empty liquor bottles and beer cans were stuffed in the trashcan. Lulu looked around the room, and Milkey offered her a chair.

"Thank you for talking with me."

"Not sure I can help."

"I'm working for a Portia Friend whose husband was killed. I'm trying to find out who killed him."

"That's what the police do, don't they?"

"Yeah, but they think it was an accident."

"They's all accidents."

"What do you mean?"

"No one ever wants to kill someone. They usually go crazy, or maybe even the person should get killed."

"How do you know?"

"Just livin' on the street, Captain, just livin' on the street."

"You know Kevin."

"I know Kevin. But, his name could be 'Bob' or 'Frank.' You never know."

"It'd be Kevin, the guy wearing the ecco's."

"I know a Kevin who wears fancy shoes, I don't know the brand."

"Didn't you notice them the first time you saw him?"

"Yep."

"Didn't you think that was odd?"

"I don't think about 'odd' on the street, Mr. Milkey. I've seen guys step outta Cadillacs and bring their packs and sacks down below the bridge."

"You don't ask their story?"

"Honey, we don't poke into anything on the street. Next thing you know, some cop is asking questions about someone you know too much about."

" I don't know the guy, but someone is concerned with the both of us. That makes me interested in Kevin. It also means that Kevin is like me, neither of us has done anything wrong."

"Whadya want from me?"

"Anything you know about him."

"He wears fancy shoes and uses big words."

"That's it?"

"Yup. And he likes peanut butter on crackers. That help any?"

"Would you be able to help me talk to him?"

Lulu squashed her nearly finished cigarette in a full ashtray on Jackson's desk. "Hell no."

"Would you do one thing for me, Lulu?"

"What."

"Would you tell him someone's tailing me. Tell him it's a new white Chevrolet Van with Maryland license plates. They're looking for him, too, at the libraries. Also, my client, Portia Friend, lost her husband, shot dead by Kansas State Highway patrolmen. Tell him she needs help."

"How come you ain't a cop anymore?"

"It didn't work out."

"Oh, you got secrets, too."

"That's right."

"I'll tell Kevin what you told me. He might leave, he might not. Now, if you're thinking you need me in the papers or in court, don't be. They's lots a places I can live. You won't find me."

"I'll keep you out of it."

"I'll see what I can do."

Chapter 49

As Don left his apartment building, he ran into Garcia at the bottom of the steps.

"Garcia."

"Good morning, boss. How you hanging?"

"I'm fine. What's up?"

"Where you going now?"

"I'm going to Walmart."

"You driving Crown Vic?"

"Yep, my Benz is in the shop."

"Benz? You have Mercedes Benz?"

"I'm joking with you."

"Oh...Benz is for rich people. Ha ha. You try to make me think you're rich. Ha. I say walk to Wal-mart."

"That'd be about ten miles, Garcia."

"Good exercise. You get healthy walking. Driving car is not so healthy."

"So long, Garcia."

"No, wait, Captain. Someone fix your car."

"You mean the window rolls down now?"

"No, someone fix your car last night. They fix your tire."

"I didn't know it was flat."

"No, boss, I mean they make it flat. It have slit in side."

Don walked up to his car. It listed to one side. The back tire on the car was flat and had a slit on the sidewall.

"Well, shit. Now I gotta change a tire."

Don took out his keys to open the trunk.

"Boss."

"What?"

"Don't open trunk."

"Is there a body in there?"

Garcia put his hand on the trunk lid. "Did you open trunk last night?"

"No."

"Someone open it last night."

"Who?"

"Person who slit tire."

"Why would he need to get in the trunk?"

"Maybe he need to put something in there."

"Like what?"

"A diversion."

"Huh?"

"Something bigger than flat tire."

Sirens approached, and flashing lights swept the area in front of Milkey's apartment building. Two squad cars pulled up, along with a tow truck, and a 2-1/2 ton truck with a reinforced box on it.

"Garcia, you think there's a bomb in my trunk?"

"I put small tape across from trunk to fender. Tape is gone. Someone open your trunk without your key. Just important smart people do that. You look at flat tire. They know you want to fix it. They know you open your trunk. I call police."

"I didn't teach you about the tape. Where'd you learn that?"

"Jesse Stone."

"What? You get your training from a detective novel?"

"I learn English, too."

The tow truck backed up to Milkey's car, a winch was hooked to the front, and the car was dragged onto the truck's platform. The back wheels, locked in position by the transmission, slide across the pavement and onto the truck's steel surface. With squad cars clearing the traffic away from the path of the tow truck, Don's 1998 Crown Victoria police interceptor was towed away.

"Garcia. You are very clever. The slit tire and the trunk, did that come from Jesse Stone?"

"No boss."
"You figured it out yourself?"
"That come from Columbo."

Chapter 50

Helen sat at Don's kitchen table while Don played the answering machine back.

"beep"

"Mr. Milkey, this is John down at Molly B's. Someone here is inquiring about you. Thought you might like to know.

"click"

"Molly B's?" Helen asked. "You still go there?"

"Not in the last year," Don said.

"Let's go check'em out."

"Okay."

Helen and Don walked down the stairs and past Don's car.

"You had a flat."

"How do you know?"

"You've got a tire on the back that's about half the size of a normal one. Your car looks like it needs a crutch."

"I guess it does."

"This a mystery to you, Don?"

"It's a long story."

"I got time."

"Someone slit my tire."

"And you changed a tire, Don? I'm impressed."

"Well, not exactly."

"Oh, I know. You had Garcia do it."

"Not exactly."

"Who did?"

"The police department."

"Why were they involved, pray tell?"

"Garcia called them."

"Why?"

"He thought there might be a bomb in the trunk. Can you imagine that?"

"And was there?"

"Crazy Garcia."

"And was there?"

"No."

"Don?"

"Not technically."

"There was a bomb."

"Just components for one. Nothing wired up."

"A bomb."

"I wouldn't call it a bomb. More likely, it was a message."

"Oh, thank goodness. Just a message that they can kill you when they want."

"I wouldn't go that far."

"Oh, Don."

They walked the four blocks to the nightlife district on Troost. Plywood covered the windows of two bars near Molly B's. One cafe displayed a dusty 'Closed' sign. Molly B's neon sign was on, but only 'Moll' was lighted. Helen and Don walked in.

"Hey, Don, long time no see," the bartender said.

"John, good to see you," Milkey said, as he walked over to the bar to shake hands. "This is my girl friend, Helen. Helen, meet John the bartender."

"How ya doin', Helen. Are you the one keeping Don away from my place?"

"I'm the one." Helen smiled. "I've got a two-block leash on him."

"My loss, your gain," John said.

"Who we meeting, John?"

"There's a lady, at least I think she's a lady, sitting in the back booth."

"Do you know her?"

"Let's just say I've seen her around. She's particularly fond of my dumpster."

"Lulu?" asked Helen.

"Don't know names. This time, though, she walked through the front door. She asked if I knew a private investigator by the name of Milk. I said 'Milkey', and she said, 'yes, that's the one.' She wanted to talk to you. I told her I hadn't seen you in a year. She said, 'you probably have his card.' And, she was right, I did."

Don looked at the back booth, but could not see who was there.

"Can I get you guys anything? It's on the house."

"Can't do it, John."

"I mean coke or water or 7-up."

"No thanks, John."

Helen and Don walked to the back of the bar. Lulu was sitting facing the back wall of the bar, and she had a drink in front of her.

"Lulu."

She turned and looked at Milkey, then at Helen.

"Who's she?"

"This is my partner Helen. Helen, meet Lulu."

Lulu moved forward in the booth and started to get up, but extended her hand instead.

"Pleased to meet you ma'am."

"Nice to meet you, Lulu."

Don and Helen sat down across from her.

"How'd you find me?"

"It wasn't easy, Captain."

"You can call me Don, Lulu. I'm not a captain."

"How did I find you? Easy. I've seen you in the neighborhood, walking to the store. I thought you might live around here."

"And frequent this bar?"

"Yes, sir."

"You've seen me in this bar?" Milkey asked as he looked at Helen.

"No I haven't. But I've seen you at the meetings."

"AA?" Helen asked.

"Yes ma'am."

"I don't recognize you," Don said.

"I was lookin' a bit better back then, about two years ago."

"You're from Kansas City?" Helen asked.

"Ain't important where I'm from."

"So, Lulu, here I am. What's this meeting about? Do you have some more information on Kevin?"

"No."

"You came in the front door at Molly B's, bought a drink, and had John call me for this meeting, and you don't have anything more on Rathbone?"

"My life don't exactly whirl around Mr. Ratbone's problems; I got other motivations in my life I need to take care of."

"And that's why we're meeting?"

Lulu fidgeted with her nearly empty drink glass.

"You see, I got people lookin' for me, too."

"Why?"

"Captain, I just want your business card, y'know? I might need some help."

"You're in trouble?"

"Don't make me tell my story. It won't do neither of us any good. I need your phone number, in case. Just in case."

Don pulled a business card from his shirt pocket and handed it to Lulu.

"Who's looking for you?"

"Don't know."

"What's your real name?"

"Lulu."

"Really?"

"Nope."

"Are you in trouble with the law?"

"Do I look like I'm in trouble with the law?"

"You know a lot about it."

"I am."

"What did you do wrong?"

Lulu finished off her drink and stood up to leave.

"I killed a man."

Chapter 51

As Helen and Don walked up to the apartments, Garcia appeared from the side of the building.

"Hey boss." Garcia placed some tools on the front step.

"Don't call me boss, Garcia."

"Okay."

"Do you have a report for me?"

"Yes, boss, I do."

"Well, what is it?"

"I have not seen white van in two days."

"How about the blue Taurus."

"I have not seen blue Taurus in five days."

"Anything else?"

"Yes, I listen to conversation on the recorder you gave me."

"What did they say?"

"You want me to play it for you?"

"Later, but tell me if they said anything important."

"They talk to someone on phone. It sound like they talk to their boss. They say they're going to homeless shelters to look for Dr. Rathbone. They ask what to do with Rathbone when they find him."

"What was said."

"They were talking on telephone. I only heard one side."

"What did they say after they asked that question?"

"They say, 'I understand'."

"Anything else?"

"He hang up, I think."

"I mean did the guys in the van have anything important to say between themselves?"

"Yes."

"Could you tell me, then, Mr. CSI."

"Yes. One said let's go to Bryant's Bar-B-Que and get some ribs."

"I meant something important, Garcia."

"Bar-B-Que not important, Captain?"

"No, I didn't say that."

"Every clue important, Boss."

"Where did you hear that, from CSI Miami?"

"No. Hercule Poirot."

"Are you taking up French now?"

"No."

Chapter 52

Bikerman pulled a sign out of the pile. It said, "Hungry, Unemployment Ran Out, Bless You For Any Help You Can Give." He grabbed his pack and the sign and took off to 6th and Broadway.

"Kevin, you got any sugar for my coffee?" Lulu asked.

Kevin looked in a side pocket of his back pack. He pulled out two packages of McDonald's sugar and handed them to her.

"Mind if I ask you somethin'?" Lulu said.

Kevin zipped up the side pocket.

"It's none of my business, I know. But maybe we could help each other."

Kevin poured some boiling water into his cup.

"I'm thinkin' you're not an ordinary homeless person."

He sipped from his cup.

"I'm not like the others either. I think you and I have a reason to be here under the bridge and crowding around the grate when it gets cold. I think we got big reasons to be here."

Kevin looked at Lulu.

"Sorry to push my nose into your business. You've never done that to me. But, I may need some help one day, and it's better that you know something about me right now."

"What's that?"

"I did something wrong a few years back."

"What was that?"

"I got real mad, and I did something I shouldn't have. Now the law is after me, and I been hiding."

He nodded.

"I think you're on the run, too, Kevin."

Kevin raised his eyebrows.

"And I don't think you're running from the law."

He looked down at his coffee cup. "How do you know that?"

"I got my ways. You got a good way of fittin' in with us, but I see a little polish on you. You don't see polish on guys here. You're different."

"Just trying to get along."

"Kevin, I came across a private eye in a bar who gave me his card, offered his help. I told him I didn't have any money, he said he could do something, pro...pro..."

"Pro bono."

"Yeah, that's it. Maybe we could meet up with him sometime."

"Not interested."

"Think about it. Maybe your situation changes and you need some help. I need some help. Who knows. Think about it."

Kevin tossed back the remainder of his coffee as the white Chevrolet van pulled up to Bikerman on the corner of 6th and Broadway.

Chapter 53

Lulu walked into Jackson's convenience store.

"Good morning, ma'am."

"Good morning. Mr. Jackson isn't it?"

"Yes."

"Just need a few things."

"Help yourself," he said.

"You got any cell phones?"

Jackson pointed over his right shoulder.

"How much?"

"$39.95, with 30 minutes of air time."

"Is that the cheapest you got?"

"Yeah. Wal-Mart has'em for $34.95, but Wal-Mart ain't here in this part of town."

"That's a lot of money for a retired lady." Lulu winked at Jackson. "Say, you know this Milkey guy?"

"He's been a customer a coupla years."

"He was a cop?"

"Yes, ma'am, he was."

"How come he's not a cop anymore?"

"That's a long story."

Lulu looked around the empty store. "I got time."

"Milkey, he used to be a patrolman around here, oh, about ten years ago. He come into my store a few times. I thought he wanted somethin' for 'protection', ya know. I didn't have anything to give him we were so broke, but he kept comin' in. Anyway, one evening, I was back in my office doing sales taxes, and two punks come in with guns pointing at my niece, who was running the cash register for me. She was 16. They wanted cash from the till. I heard yellin' and screamin' and shootin'. I was back there doin' taxes. I should've been at the cash register. That's all it took, a few seconds. I go out to see my niece sittin' in her own blood. She not movin'.

"The front door opened and Milkey and his partner come in with guns pulled. I ducked down behind a stack of soda cases. After the shooting stopped, Milkey's partner leaned against the refrigeration cases, blood dripping from his left hand. One punk was dead and the other dying. Cap'm, he look at me and tell me to go back in my office and call the police. I did what he said. I heard one last shot. When I got back from my office, Milkey was helping his partner. The second punk was dead. He had a hole in the back of his head."

"Which one did it?"

"His partner, Mr. Doherty, died at the hospital. The final report say he did it. But, Cap'm, he change the report. Said he did it. News got out, and the community went wild. They wanted Milkey fired, and he was."

"So, which one did it? Whose gun was used?"

"Don't know. Report say he was shot dead by an unregistered gun. Could've been Milkey's or Doherty's."

"Or yours."

Jackson looked down at the floor. "I have a gun, Miss Lulu. I had it that night. My story ends here, but I'll tell you somethin'. I calls Mr. Milkey 'Cap'm' sometimes, sometimes 'General.' But when no one's around 'cept my family and friends, maybe we sittin' around the Sunday dinner table and Cap'm's name come up, we don't call him 'Cap'm,' we call him 'Judge'. If you asking if he treat you right, that's my answer."

Lulu paid the $4.76 and left the store with a sack large enough to hold a half-pint of whiskey and a cell phone.

Chapter 54

Lulu saw the white van pull to a stop a block away from the 6th and Wyandotte bridge. She stood up and kicked Kevin's boot.

"Kevin, you got to go."

"What?"

"Get your pack, and get outta here."

"Why?"

"See that white van up there?"

"Yeah?"

"I seen it before. It's a brand new Chevrolet Van with Maryland license plates. Up close, it got little tiny antennae on the side."

Kevin stared at the van as two men emerged.

"It's got tinted windows all around. It's a van owned by people with money to spend. You got any ideas about them people, Kevin?"

Kevin packed his backpack and rolled up his sleeping bag. "Yep," said Kevin.

"Kevin."

"Yeah?"

"Don't take any bus or plane out of town. They'll be at the terminal. Don't rent a car, they're all over that. Don't go to the homeless shelters. Meet me at Jackson's store at 6:00 tonight. Now, pick up a sign and walk away from here."

Kevin grabbed a sign. "Thanks, Lulu." He walked away.

The two men arrived at the campsite as Kevin disappeared under the bridge at Broadway. The short man glanced at the bridge.

"Morning ma'am, we're looking for my brother, Kevin. He's been hanging out around here. You know him?"

"Oh, I know several Kevin's, but they're not real names."

"Well, he's got mental problems, ya know? He's a scientist, and he'd be wearing more expensive clothes. Seen anyone like that?"

"We're all kinda touched in the head down here. And we all come across fancy boots and scarves in the trash. Look at this scarf I got. Here, look at it. It's pure wool. About seventy-five bucks on a Nordstrom rack, I'd reckon. What do you think?"

"Thanks ma'am, we'll be moving on." He nodded to the big man and motioned in the direction Kevin had taken.

Lulu stepped in their way. She pulled a book from her coat pocket. It was the King James's version of the Bible.

"Out of our way, Lady, we're gonna find Kevin today, and we don't need any preaching from a homeless person." The big man pushed her aside.

"Ya'll believe in the power of prayer? Maybe that would help in finding this Kevin."

"Get a job, bitch. Maybe the Lord will write you a letter of reference." Said the short man as they walked past her.

The two men were twenty feet away from Lulu. The sound behind them was metal sliding against metal, and then a 'snap.' They stopped at once and turned around together. The clip was in the gun. The gun was in her hand. It was pointed at them.

"Gentlemen, I'm a god-fearing Christian, and I believe in prayer, but I know the Lord has a lot on his hands. Sometime my prayers stack up on Him, and they ain't answered as quick as I need them to be answered. I'm sure that's why he told me to buy a gun, not one that would hold just six shells, but one with a big clip, cause he didn't want me to have to pray that each bullet would shoot straight. Now, I'm praying here that you two gentlemen will go back up that hill and get into your truck and drive away. I'm thinking God might be busy right now with some soo-nam-ee on the other side of the world out of earshot of my prayer. I believe I'm in charge now, and I'm asking you, in the Lord's name, to get back to your van."

"Do you even know where the trigger is on that thing, lady?"

"I'm asking you polite now, to get in your van and don't look back."

Lulu swung the gun around and pointed at the van. She slowly squeezed the trigger. One second passed, another and another and then the gun fired and recoiled, Lulu's hands and arms absorbing the opposite force from the bullet heading towards the van. The passenger rearview mirror broke into tiny pieces, most of them falling to the ground.

"God would say to be nice to the lady. He would want you to go now," she said, directing her gun back to the intruders.

"Yes'm," said the big guy.

Chapter 55

Milkey walked into the small office with the name "Sandra Schmidt" taped next to the doorway.

"Mr. Milkey, have a seat," said Ms. Schmidt. "Coffee?"

"No thanks."

"You recall we had a conversation about John Billingsley, the police chief of Kearney?"

"Yup."

"And my notes tell me you're working for Portia Friend, the wife of the former Kearney police chief."

"Right."

"He was shot and killed by Kansas Highway Patrolmen, wasn't he?"

"Yes, he had some violations showing up in the database, including armed robbery."

"But he was a law enforcement officer."

"Yeah."

"The violations were wrong?"

"That's right."

"Mr. Milkey, don't you wonder how wrong information can get on a record like that?"

"I do."

"I talked to Cassidy, who was assigned to investigate the case."

"And..."

"Cassidy said KCPD was asked to help, given that Kearney was in such disarray."

"Makes sense."

"Cassidy said it was a case of mistaken identity."

"No shit."

"He said he closed the case."

"I see."

"What do you think about that?" Ms. Schmidt asked.

"I think you don't believe him," said Milkey. "You think there's more to the case, and you want to write about it."

"Is there more to the case? Do you still work for Portia Friend?"

"Yup."

"And your job is to look for her husband's killer?"

"It is."

"Mr. Milkey. Could you be just a little bit more informative than 'yes' or 'no'?"

"Nope."

"You believe there's someone else involved in Chief Friend's death."

"Ms. Schmidt, maybe I can save you some time. You and I work for different purposes. It's possible we could combine our time and efforts, but I don't think this is the best time to do that. Cassidy closed the case. I haven't. That's what you know. Who you believe is your job."

"I don't believe anybody until I put pen to paper. I do research until I come to a conclusion. I've done research on you. I know you used to be a policeman. Now you aren't. Something happened, and now you're a private detective. That something had Cassidy's name all over it. Am I right?"

Milkey looked out the window of the small office.

"I am right," she said.

"Right or wrong, it isn't important."

"I think it is."

"It was ten years ago."

"Killing a kid goes away after ten years?"

Milkey grasped the arms of the chair and stood up. He looked straight at her. "Ms. Schmidt, I'm still working for Mrs. Friend. Maybe something you have will help me, and I'd appreciate knowing what you have. I can't help you right now because I'm still investigating. The kid? He doesn't affect this case. I forget where he was in the store. I haven't thought twice about him. I do remember the 16-year old girl behind the cash register. I remember the pool of blood she sat in, the exact color of red. I remember the pack of Winston-Salem cigarettes that had fallen off the shelf and landed in the pool of blood, and stood on its end, as if someone placed it there. Here's how ten years ago affects this case: I'm thinking that if I can find who killed John Friend, maybe that cigarette pack that I saw last night, three days ago, four days ago, and probably tomorrow, will go away. Probably not, but it's worth a shot. Keep in touch, Ms Schmidt."

Chapter 56

"What's this?" Garcia asked.

"It's pay for helping me," Don said.

"I thought I am prenticeshipman."

"Apprentice," Helen said.

"Apprenticeshipman."

"You're not, Garcia. You're my assistant. You're paid. Not much, but you're paid."

"Thank you, boss, I have report for you."

"All right. Let's hear it."

"It's on your phone box."

Helen, Don and Garcia went into Don's apartment. Don pressed the replay button.

Beep.

"Hey, Don. This is Frank. You're a busy man. We haven't seen you for many weeks. Come on down to the meeting this Thursday. We all want to know how you're doing. Seven o'clock. See you. God loves you, and so do I."

Click.

Beep.

"Mr. Milkey, this is Sandra Schmidt with the Star. Call me.

Click.

Beep.

"Mr. Milkey, this is Bryan Lewis with Crown Refinance. We've got a great deal to help you lower your interest rates on your credit card down to 2.7%. Return my call to hear about this great offer."

Click.

Beep.

"5:30 tonight. Meet me where we met last time."

Click.

"She's not very informative," Helen said. "You got someone on the side, Don?"

"It's Lulu."

"Who's Lulu?"

"She's a homeless person."

"A homeless person with phone?" Garcia asked.

"Sure. Maybe she's using a public phone."

"Where that be, boss?"

"They're all around."

"I don't think so, Don. Maybe in the 1970's, but not today," said Helen.

"Maybe we need to rethink this. Rathbone is the scientist who is hiding out with the homeless people. But, Lulu said she was running from something, no doubt it had to do with something about her killing someone. She's on the run, too. But she's reaching out for help from me. And she knows Rathbone. Maybe we can get more information at 5:30."

"Maybe so, chief."

"Don't call me chief, Garcia."

"No problem."

"Maybe she's a sensitive woman, and she just wants to help the guy," said Helen.

"At risk to her self?" asked Don.

"It's been known to happen," said Helen.

"Maybe for some deep self interest,"

"I'm sorry, I misspoke," said Helen. "Maybe she's a sensitive woman, and she just wants to help the guy. It's been known to happen...you moron."

Chapter 57

Helen and Don entered Molly B's. Don waved at John. John waved back and pointed to the back of the bar. Lulu sat in the booth, hidden from view from the front of the bar. Don and Helen sat down.

"You've got a gun," Don said.

"How do you know?" Lulu asked.

" It's been fired. I can smell the sulphur."

"That's right. I had to protect Kevin today. The guys in the white van came by and started to chase Kevin. I had to step in."

"Anyone hurt?"

"No, I just shot their van. For demonstration purposes."

"They didn't believe you could handle a gun?"

"They didn't. But now Kevin's got no place to go."

"Does he have money?"

"I don't know, but it wouldn't do him any good. I warned him not to go to the bus terminal or the airport. I told him to come to Jackson's store at 6:00."

"You think he'll come?"

"I think he's got no place to go, and he's going to need someone," Lulu said.

"Jackson has a little office in the back. We can talk to him there."

"Fine. You and Helen go on in first before six. I'll be in the store. It's important that he trust us. I've mentioned you, but that's about all."

Chapter 58

"I guess a gal can't smoke in here, even if she is nervous as hell," said Lulu, her right hand clutching a pack of cigarettes.

Jackson's office contained no ashtray, and the table top had cigarette burn scars left by smokers having no need for one.

"How do you know my name?" Kevin asked, directing his question to Don.

"The same people who have been searching for you have been following me."

"The guys in the white van?"

"Yes."

"How did you know they were looking for me?"

"We overheard their conversation."

"You bugged their van?"

"Yes."

"How did you find me? Did you follow their van?"

"No, we just shop in the same store you do."

"You mean this one we're in now," Kevin said.

"Yup."

"That's your search technique? Shopping in neighborhood stores?"

"We call it 'keeping our eyes and ears open'," Don said.

Helen interrupted. "You were a homeless person wearing expensive shoes."

"Ah yes, I couldn't give up my comfortable shoes. But the big question is why the same people are following you and I."

"You'd make a good detective."

"How's that?"

"You're asking the right questions."

"I don't have much else to do. I'm being tracked down by men in a van that has Maryland license plates. I'll bet if you looked closer, you'd find that van is from the county that contains Ft. Meade. That's the home of the National Security Agency. These guys don't work for NSA, but I bet they did at one time. There's a community of skills around that place, and there are people for hire."

"What is the National Security Agency?" asked Lulu.

"They are codemakers and codebreakers, and surveillance is their middle name. I thought you were dead, Lulu, I heard a shot."

"You probably didn't think a woman would be carrying a gun, nor she'd be doing some shootin'."

"No Lulu, I didn't think a homeless person would be carrying a gun."

"I shot their car."

"You shot their car? Why?"

"To show'em I knew how to use it."

"Why?"

"I told you. So they'd believe me."

"No, Lulu, I want to know why you did that for me? Why did you take a chance for someone you don't hardly know?"

Lulu fumbled with her pack of cigarettes.

"Maybe she wants to help you." Helen said.

"She wants to help a virtual stranger?" Kevin said.

"Maybe things aren't so black and white in her world as they are in yours."

"How do you know about my world?"

"Dr. Rathbone, you're an open book to me," Helen said. "You're a computer geek; you're on the run from people who will break your knee-caps when they find you, maybe more. You've got a bunch of cash, and a pile of fear. You're worrying where you're gonna to sleep tonight because the bridges and the shelters aren't safe anymore. And, because you are a rational and logical man, you're wondering what we all have in common that is of interest to some guys playing CIA in the Midwest."

"NSA," Don said.

"Is she your partner?" Rathbone asked.

"She is."

"She's right," Kevin said. "I'm wondering who you are and what your interest is in me."

"I'm Don Milkey. I'm a private investigator."

"Okay."

"I represent a woman named Portia Friend who recently lost her husband."

"And, somehow I'm linked to her losing her husband?"

"No. Mrs. Friend's husband was killed. I'm investigating his murder. He was the police chief of Kearney, Missouri."

"I'm looking for something we share, Mr. Milkey. I don't see it."

"I don't either."

"Perhaps you could tell us something about yourself," Helen said.

"I'm from Denver."

"Yeah, is that it?" Helen asked.

"No. I'm a computer scientist."

"I think we've...." Helen said before she was interrupted by Don.

"Who do you work for? Don asked.

"Innovative Software Solutions."

"Kevin, I don't think you work for them anymore," Lulu said.

"Nope."

"What does Innovative Software Solutions do, Kevin?" Helen asked.

"They're software developers for the banking industry."

"What kind of software do they develop?"

"They sell a product called 'Smart Shield'." It is a security system that prevents intruders from accessing financial accounts. Internally, we call it 'panther'."

"You wrote it," said Helen.

"Not exactly. I designed it. It was written by a team of developers who worked for me."

"How come you don't work for them anymore?"

"I found something wrong with the program."

"You couldn't fix it?"

"Yes, I could."

"So, what was the problem?"

"Under certain circumstances, Panther was blocking customer access, mistaking them for hackers. I recommended they shut down the systems immediately, find the bug, fix it, and then re-install the systems."

"And..."

"My boss, Brent Iverson, said they would fix it on the fly, so as not to alarm our customers. I said it needed to be uninstalled. He said I wasn't working on the system anymore anyway. It was not my concern. I said it was unethical to not inform our customers."

"What did he say to that?"

"He didn't. He just called in Thornton Hopkins, the chief of security."

"What did this Hopkins say?"

"He said he needed my keys and my badge, and he said he and his two buddies would accompany me to my desk so they could observe me as I cleaned out my desk."

"It's a software company, they're not drug smugglers or the Mafia. What's the threat?" Helen asked.

Kevin slowly shook his head, and then looked at Milkey.

"This Hopkins guy, he's a serious person. From the first day I met him, I knew he wasn't just a high paid security guard. He's in the business of security. When they walked me to the door that day, he told me I would be in danger if I got in their way."

"Did you get in his way?" Milkey asked.

"Yep. I went to the president of the first bank where we installed Smart Shield. It was the Bank of Caspar, in Caspar, Wyoming."

"What happened?"

"The bank president told me he'd check with his IT people. I called him the next day, and my call was routed to his voice mail. Same thing the next day, and the next."

"So?" Don asked.

"Hopkins probably stepped in and described me as some paranoid ex-employee who was trying to make some money off Innovative Solutions."

"On the basis of that, you think your life is in danger?" Milkey asked.

"Think? Think? I know Hopkins and his type. In the security business, you can't tolerate uncertainty. I'm his loose cannon."

"But, if something happened to you, surely an investigation would eventually lead to Innovative Solutions. Even if nothing could be proven, they couldn't afford to tarnish their reputation, like a top scientist fired from their company turning up dead somewhere."

"You don't understand, Milkey. I may not turn up. They have power that you can't fathom. If they're tailing you, you should be worried, too."

"Why would they be watching me?" asked Milkey.

Rathbone sat up in his chair. "Beats the hell out of me." The computer scientist stood up and pushed his chair to the table. "Thanks for the chat. I've got to go now."

"Where you going to stay tonight, Kevin?" Lulu asked.

"I'll find a place."

"Don't come back to our camp. They'll be there."

"I know."

"Dr. Rathbone, wait," Helen said. "We're investigating the death of a police chief. He was shot by Kansas State Highway patrolmen."

"Sounds like you've found the killers," said Rathbone, as he left the room.

Chapter 59

Rachel Rathbone sat at a conference table in the Morrison, Colorado police station. On the table was a handwritten letter.

"Mrs. Rathbone, you don't know me, but I hope I can gain your trust. I am Don Milkey, a private investigator in Kansas City. I represent a client whose husband was killed on Interstate 70, outside of Topeka, Kansas. His name was John Friend. In the course of my investigation, I have crossed paths with your husband, Kevin. I don't know if you are in touch with him, but I thought it might be possible that you aren't, and you are worrying about him. I assure you he is all right and is safe. I know where he is, but I will tell no one. I would like to meet with you at a time and location of your choosing. I would think you'd want to meet in a public place. Please write back to my post office box. I am the only one who has access to it. I'm looking forward to meeting you.
Signed, Don Milkey."

The door of the conference room opened, and a police sergeant ushered in Milkey. He wore a sport jacket and a tie. The design on the tie only partially hid a ketchup stain.

"Do you want me to stay, Mrs. Rathbone?"

"No, sergeant, please close the door."

"Are you friends with the police department?"

"No, but they're small town and helpful to a stranger. How do I know you're Don Milkey, and more importantly, how do I know you have my best interests at heart?"

"You don't. You'll just have to listen to my story, and then decide for yourself. You know, Mrs. Rathbone, I have to trust you, too."

"I don't understand."

"I told Kevin I would keep anything he told me confidential."

"I'm his wife."

"In my business, Mrs. Rathbone, that's not enough."

"Tell me, Mr. Milkey, is Kevin growing a beard?"

"Yes."

"Tell me about it."

"It's not a full beard. There are some spots on the left side of his face that are not generating hair."

"Mr. Milkey, Kevin has been threatened by his employer. That's why he's on the run."

"Kevin has told me that. He's also mentioned Thornton Hopkins."

"Oh, geez, Mr. Milkey, Kevin is so smart and knowledgeable, but he sees good in people to a fault."

"What do you mean?"

"He was happy to go to work for Innovative Solutions. He was taken by Iverson and Hopkins. They had a vision, not just a company, Kevin said. He thought his software team was so brilliant. Then we had everyone over for a company picnic early on, so we could get to know each other."

"You didn't see the vision?"

"Mr. Milkey, they walked into our house, each one waving a red flag completely invisible to Kevin. Iverson was so slick he dripped grease on the carpet when I shook his hand. Hopkins, the security man, was so much in charge I wondered how Kevin could miss it. Mazzoli is an evangelist, not a marketer. And the software team? I've been around computer scientists. I've had parties where Kevin invited all the smart guys from Carnegie-Mellon. Believe me, Innovative Solutions hired one computer scientist, my husband, Kevin, and then they hired five computer thugs without a bachelor's degree among them. No doubt they were brilliant with computer code, but abject failures at social code. When they all left, Kevin was beaming. I only smiled back.

"Mrs. Rathbone, someone is trying to interfere with my investigation of John Friend's murder. They've staked me out, assaulted my assistant, and planted a fake bomb in the trunk of my car. We bugged their stake-out vehicle and overheard their discussion of their strategy to find your husband. In my opinion, John Friend and Kevin Rathbone are linked."

"More specifically, John Friend and Thornton Hopkins are linked."

"And Iverson."

Mrs. Rathbone nodded. "Mr. Milkey, I hope you can protect Kevin."

"I've got my best people on the job."

"They're not tougher than Hopkins."

"That remains to be seen," Milkey said. "My money is on the good guys."

Chapter 60

Milkey parked his car on Quinten St. at 16th, in downtown Denver. Innovative Software Solutions' office occupied the eighth floor of the seventeen-story Mercantile Building at that address. Don locked his car and buttoned his sport coat, hiding the .38 Smith & Wesson revolver. He looked one more time at the photograph of Brent Iverson, CEO of the software company, then stuffed in into his coat pocket. At 11:30 a.m, Milkey took a seat at a table in the first floor cafeteria. He waited. Two men, one of them Iverson, went through the cashier line and then took a seat across the cafeteria from Milkey.

Milkey approached the two men.

"Gentlemen," Don said.

The men looked up.

"Can we help you with something?" Iverson asked.

Don grabbed a chair at the table, pulled it out and sat down.

"I'm glad we all could meet this morning," Don said.

Hopkins looked at Iverson.

"Who are you?" Brent asked.

"Don Milkey." Don looked at Iverson, then Hopkins. "I'm a private investigator from Kansas City."

"You're a ways from home," Hopkins said.

"You must be Thornton Hopkins, chief of security."

Hopkins did not reply.

"How can we help you before we enjoy our lunch," Iverson said.

"I'm investigating a murder."

"A murder? How on earth is that related to us?"

"I'm investigating a Dr. Kevin Rathbone, a former member of your staff."

"Yes?"

"He's a former member of your staff, am I correct?" Don said.

"We generally don't talk about personnel matters, especially with strangers," Hopkins said.

" As I understand it, he disagreed with you on how to handle a bug in the program he was developing. He wanted to bring the whole system down, and you wanted to fix it on the fly. Do I have that right?"

"Not really your business," Hopkins said.

"Who got murdered?" Iverson asked.

"John Friend, the police chief of Kearney, Missouri."

"Sorry to hear about that," said Iverson. "How do we fit in?"

"John friend was pulled over on I-70 west of Topeka. His records showed sixteen traffic tickets, and warrants for his arrest for armed robbery. When he held up his badge to show the patrolmen, they thought he was drawing on them, so they opened fire."

"Geez, what a pity," Iverson said. "And you think we can help in some way?"

"Yes I do. I think John Friend was onto you guys, and you altered his database records."

"Uh, Brent," said Hopkins.

Iverson continued. "Ha! You're in a fantasy land, Milkey. You need to take your little theories back to Kansas City and play police detective in your own neighborhood. I know your kind, Milkey," said Iverson.

Hopkins interrupted. "Brent."

Iverson continued. "You couldn't make it in real law enforcement, so you got yourself some business cards and a phone and became a private eye. Sixteen parking tickets? Ha! You ought to be in some detective novel," said Iverson.

"Brent, this is over," Hoplins said.

"Parking tickets?" Milkey asked.

"What..." said Iverson.

Hopkins pushed away from the table and stood up.

"I said, 'sixteen traffic violations', you said 'sixteen parking tickets'," said Milkey.

"We're done here," Hopkins said, moving over to Milkey. "Where you parked?"

Hopkins guided Milkey out of the cafeteria and down the street towards his car.

"Milkey, you've stepped into something here you don't want to be standing in, I'm telling you."

"What have I stepped into? asked Milkey.

"You're in outta your league. You need to go home and watch soap operas or whatever else you do when you're not playing private eye."

"Is that a threat?"

"To say the least."

"Here's mine, Hopkins. You need to shut down your software and your threats. If you don't, your name will be on the front page of the Kansas City Star and it will be picked up by any other interested media."

"Ha! Milkey, you just made my point. You don't know shit," said Hopkins. "Try and see if you can have a nice day."

———

"Iverson, could you, just for once, keep your fuckin' mouth shut?" Hopkins said as he sat back down at the cafeteria table.

"What, I don't understand, traffic tickets, parking tickets, what's the deal?"

"We've got some trouble, now."

"He's just a two-bit PI, Hopkins."

"A two-bit PI? A two-bit PI? You don't have a clue, Iverson."

"We have lunch, he shows up and makes a charge he can't substantiate, you usher him out. What's the big deal?"

"The big deal is we didn't have lunch, we had a meeting."

"Whatever you want to call it, you emailed us to come down here, we bought food, we talked."

"That's it, Brent. You don't know shit. You haven't a clue how Milkey happened to show up at our table. I didn't email you, you didn't email me; how'd we get here?"

"You didn't email me?"

"No. Open your fuckin' eyes, Iverson. We just had a meeting called by a two-bit PI."

"Huh?"

"He's met with Rathbone for sure. He's in our system," Hopkins yelled. "He planned this meeting, came in to discover our link to John Friend, got it, and then left."

"He's not that smart."

"We're in fucking trouble. We're going to have to wind it up."

"We haven't met our goal yet."

"Yeah, let's wait for more money so that we'll be able to afford the best lawyers."

"We can't give up because of some half-assed PI."

"You don't get what I just said, Brent. I hired you to be our corporate face, and you've done a good job of that behind your big shiny desk. But they didn't teach you how to handle the curve ball in business school, and your view of things just failed us. Brent, I've been in this business for thirty years. That ketchup spot on Milkey's tie, you see that as weakness. But to me, I've seen lots of spotless ties. I know those guys by their perfect $75 ties and their tailored suits. But this guy Milkey, he's a loose cannon Colombo type that I can't predict except for one thing, and it ain't good. I can tell you, down the road, if I have to offer the guy money for his silence, there won't be any number of zeroes I can put on the check that will get him to take it. You wonder why I'm bringing this project down? It's precisely because of the guy who drives a car made in the previous century, the guy with the frayed cuffs on his coat. I know this business. He's motivated by who knows what, but not by money. We start shutting down right now."

Chapter 61

"Where are you now? Helen asked.

"I'm about halfway, Hays, Kansas," Don said.

"How come you didn't tell me you were going?"

"I didn't want you to worry."

"Worry? Worry? Don, worry is good. It keeps a person from getting killed."

"Our meeting was public."

"Oh, that reassures me. Lulu had a public meeting with some bad guys and that didn't stop those guys from being shot at."

"She shot the van."

"Oh, I forgot that little difference. In Denver, they're probably more discrete with their shootings. I feel fine, now."

"Great."

"Whatdja find out?"

"They are linked to John Friend's death."

"How did you find that out?"

"I told them they were, and they didn't deny it. They also knew about the parking tickets."

"But you didn't know they were linked."

"No, but I do now."

"Don?"

"Yes?"

"Could I ask you something personal?"

"I've never been able to stop you before."

"No, this is real personal."

"Give it a shot."

"Okay, now don't think this is silly."

"I won't."

"Okay...here it is. Would you have gone to Denver without telling me, if we were married?"

"Now that's silly."

"No, Don, please. I'm serious."

"The answer would be 'no'."

"So a little marriage certificate would make that big a change?"

"Yes."

"I don't understand. You're so disinterested in paperwork and red tape and conventional ways of doing things. We've got such a great relationship; we color outside the lines, we are so outside the box, you don't keep receipts, you park in handicapped slots, you always go seventy-five in a seventy. You're doing that right now, I'll bet. Aren't you?"

"Remind me not to be so predictable."

"So what's a little piece of paper?"

"It's not the paper."

"What is it, then?"

"It's the words we say."

"Okay, I get it. Don?"

"Yes?"

"Try me again. Ask me again."

"I can't."

"Is there another woman?"

"Yes."

"I understand. It's Portia Friend. You've made a commitment to her."

"Yes."

"When this is over, Don, try me again. I need to know what trouble you're getting yourself into. If I don't know, I speculate. Believe me my worries go sky high; I'd rather have the truth."

"Uncle Don, this is Jake."

"Hi, Jake."

"Your cell has been off."

"I've been talking to Helen. What's up?"

"You've been in Denver?"

"How did you know?"

"Because that's where you picked up three parking tickets."

Chapter 62

"Garcia, what happened?"

"My face, it got in front of someone's fist."

"And your leg?"

"It got in front of someone's foot."

"Who were they?"

"Your friends."

"My friends?"

"Yes, the men in the blue van."

"Blue? Not white? The same men?"

"I don't know. But there were four of them."

"What did they look like?"

"One, the big strong one, he was the one in the white van. I did not see the shorter man from the white van. They were standing outside your apartment. The hall light was off. I ask them if I could help them. They didn't say anything. They just beat me up."

"Did they say something after that?"

"Yes."

"What."

"I couldn't understand them. They were speaking in Russian."

"They're Russian?"

"No, boss, I did not say they were Russian. I say they spoke Russian."

"So they weren't Russian."

"That's right. They were not good at Russian. They used English words when their Russian was not good enough."

Milkey reached for the bulb in the hallway. It was loose in its socket. He screwed it back in to light the hallway.

"Let's get you into my apartment."

"I'm ok, boss."

"Don't call me boss, Garcia."

"Okay, boss."

Milkey helped Garcia to the recliner next to the table upon which sat the answering machine with one message on it.

"Beep."

"Meet me where we met before. Three o'clock. I have some questions."

"Click."

"Who's that, boss?"

"That's Rathbone."

Chapter 63

"Who's the kid with the laptop?" Kevin asked.

"He's my nephew, Jake."

"Some kinda computer whiz?"

"Nah, I'm really a biology major; I do computers on the side," Jake said.

"What are you using for an operating system?"

"I use them all."

"Why do you need more than one?"

"It's important when I'm doing serious hacking."

"You'll have to tell me about that. I'm in the business."

"Dr. Rathbone, you said you had some questions," Milkey said.

"Yes. I got to thinking about how highway patrolmen would accidentally shoot a police chief. They must have thought him to be a threat."

"Yes. He had a large number of parking violations and was being sought for killing two off-duty policemen in a robbery attempt."

"And, they weren't accurate computer records."

"No."

"Where'd they come from?"

"There was no source noted."

"No doubt," Rathbone said. "My dissertation was on database design. Security is a large part of that field. The easiest method would be to bypass the transaction entry system and just change a record."

"Could someone at Innovative Solutions do that?"

Kevin didn't answer immediately.

"Could it be Hopkins?"

"No. How do you know Hopkins?"

"I met with him."

"What?"

"After you left our last meeting, I went to Denver, had a meeting with Hopkins and Iverson."

"How did you have a meeting with those guys? You just can't dial 'em up and meet for lunch."

"Yes, you can. But I used their e-mail. I had them meet in the cafeteria."

"But they wouldn't go to lunch on the request of a stranger."

"They wouldn't. But I had Paul Mazzoli, your VP of marketing, call the meeting."

"You'd have to know Mazzoli's password to do that."

"Correct."

Rathbone looked at Jake.

"You got him the password."

"That's right."

"How did you do it?"

"I googled his name. Went to every hit and compiled a list of names and numbers. The first names of his immediate family, the names of his pets, street addresses where he lived or worked. Street numbers, zip codes, phone numbers. Then I used a little program that tries all combinations. I settled on PAMazzoli as the username, and turned the program loose on the password. It hit on its eleventh try, 'matilda' his daughter's name."

"The E-mail system blocks you after the third try. You couldn't get to the eleventh try."

"True. The program I use is little, but it's powerful. If it gets blocked, it tries to log back in through another browser, and if it still is blocked, it reboots to another operating system and continues its attempts. Innovative Solutions e-mail system was solved by Windows 7, the Opera browser."

"Where you going to school, Jake?"

"Free State."

"Where's that?"

"Lawrence, Kansas."

"Never heard of that college."

"It's a high school."

"I should have known you don't get that kind of knowledge at a university. What did you find out in your meeting, Milkey?"

"Several things. Hopkins recognized me."

"He probably had photos from his men here in Kansas City."

"I found out Hopkins is in charge, not Iverson."

"I didn't know that, but it doesn't surprise me."

"And, Iverson knew about John Friend's parking violations."

"No shit. Why would he tell you?"

"He didn't. I deduced it. What's Mazzoli's role?"

"He's their vice-president of marketing. He wasn't around much. I guess he was on the road selling Smart Shield."

"Enough about me, Kevin. What do you make of all this?"

Kevin took a drink from his coffee cup.

"Usually when you finish a project, the development team disbands, or at least it slims down. When Smart Shield was completed and installed in ten banks, all five of the guys working for me were still working for Innovative Solutions. Iverson said they were moving into customer support positions. That was the beginning of the end of our relationship when I told Brent that we would have the world's smartest and most expensive support team. He said he wasn't taking any chances. I knew he was lying. I suspected then that these computer scientists were there for another reason."

"What would that reason be?"

"I don't know, but hacking the police database would fit their talents."

"Why would they do that?"

"I don't know. Maybe Jake knows."

"Nope," said Jake. "I've read all of Iverson's emails, and they don't reveal much of anything."

"They wouldn't. Under Hopkins orders, we never communicated anything about Smart Shield, unless we were in a meeting in the safe room on the eighth floor."

"Jake, could you get into Iverson's mail and search on 'John Friend'?"

"Yes."

"Let me know this afternoon what you find."

"How about now?"

"You got a signal here in the ghetto?"

"Yup. It's 'uspo117'."

"That's the post office down the street. Isn't it secured by password?"

"I'll search the email for 'Friend'."

"How did you blow by that password?" asked Rathbone.

"One of my friends discovered the algorithm for the password for U.S. Post Office wireless connections. When you drive down the street, you can log into Starbucks, McDonalds, and now, all U.S. Post offices."

"You have friends smarter than you?"

"Well, we call each other friends, but we're just strangers meeting on the internet. I don't find 'Friend', uncle Don."

"Thanks, Jake. Could you write down the URL for the email system? I'd like to read Iverson's mail."

"Okay. But there are about three thousand emails with another two thousand in the trash. This could take a lot of your time."

"I need to read them."

"How about searching on some key words?" Jake asked.

"Like what?"

"Try 'fuck you'."

"That'd be interesting."

"Okay, here you go. It's to Martha Iverson, his wife, as I recall from my research. It says he's sorry he can't get back home for another three weeks. He says Smart Shield is in the middle of a launch. Say's he loves her."

"And where is the 'fuck you'?"

"That was her reply."

"Hey, this is good. How about a word that would indicate some emotions. Like 'moron'."

"Will do."

"Is this what small-time PI's do? Pardon my characterization," Rathbone said.

"Yup. We don't pass up any small-time enjoyment."

"Here you go, Uncle Don. It's an email from Iverson to kccap at yahoo. It says: 'Call me, you fucking moron. You know the number'."

"Hmmm."

"It was a reply to kccap. The original says: 'Milkey too dumb to be a problem. Cassidy.' It was in Iverson's trash bin."

Chapter 64

"What's on your mind, Mr. Milkey? Do you have a story for me for the front page?" Sandra Schmidt asked.

"Can we talk in private?"

Sandra motioned Don over to an empty office and shut the door. "What's up?"

"I'm just trying to lay some groundwork here."

"Concerning..."

"John Friend."

"What about him. Do you have some information on him?"

"Yes."

"Well?"

"I can't tell you."

"You came here to tell me you can't tell me?"

"Yes. Have you been in touch with Cassidy?"

"Yes."

"What did he have to say?"

"This is laying the 'groundwork'?"

"Bear with me."

"They're closing the case on John Friend. It was an accident."

"Are you okay with that?"

"Unless you've got some special information to give me today."

"I do. Did you know John Friend had sixteen parking violations?"

"Yes."

"And a robbery warrant?"

"Yes."

"Are you interested where they came from?"

"I assumed the chief of police of Kearney, Missouri, would not rack up sixteen parking tickets all by himself. According to his wife, the first one was legitimate."

"So, where did the rest of them come from?"

"A mistake in the database software."

"Is that what Cassidy told you?"

"Yes."

"You believe him?"

"No. I'm a reporter."

"Someone put them there."

"Who? I deal in names, Milkey."

"I don't know."

"That's it? That's the information you have for me?"

"I'm investigating this for Mrs. Friend. All I want to know is if you'd be willing to report a story if I brought it to you?"

"Maybe. It depends on the story. What's the story?"

"It's about who put the parking violations in the database."

"Milkey, do you know the names?"

"Yes."

"Absolutely, are you sure?"

"Almost."

"Give me a hint."

"You need to keep after Cassidy."

"He did it?"

"I didn't say that."

"You want me to pressure him."

"You might...maybe...yes."

"Could you be more specific with what you know about Cassidy?"

"I think he's covering up something."

Schmidt put down her pen.

"Mr. Milkey, If I understand you correctly, you want me to help with your investigation."

"I prefer to call it me helping you."

"For a man who follows the direct approach, you sure are the weasel today."

"There are degrees of directness."

"I'm sure."

Milkey unfolded a piece of paper he had in his shirt pocket. He pushed it over to Ms. Schmidt.

"What's this?"

"It's information on a Brent Iverson, who is the chief executive officer for Innovative Solutions in Denver. That's his office phone number."

"And?"

"Call him."

"What would we be talking about?"

"Anything you want."

"Should I use your name and Cassidy's?"

"Sure."

"I'm not used to doing research unprepared."

"I do it all the time."

"No shit, Milkey."

"I call it the direct approach."

Chapter 65

Beep.

"Mr. Milkey. This is Henry Gonzalez, chief of police for the city of Randolph, Missouri. I need to talk to you."

Click.

Garcia awoke from a nap in Don's chair. "Somebody just call, boss?"

"Yup."

"You no answer it?"

"Nope."

" If I call you on this phone and you sit next to it when I call, will you answer it?"

"No. How are you feeling, Garcia?"

"I feel fine. You should be more professional. You have PI business. When people call, you say, 'hello, how may I direct your call?'. Or better, 'Milkey and Associates, how may I direct your call?"

"What if they wanted to talk to me?"

"You say, 'one moment please.' Then you put your hand over the phone, wait a bit, then say, 'This is Don Milkey, how can I help you?' "

"I'd have to change my voice. Otherwise they'd know I was the same person as the receptionist."

"That's right, chief. You do good with this business."

"Garcia. Check it out. There's only two of us. We're not a big business."

"Oh no, boss. When we surround the criminals, we don't say, 'hey, come on out with your hands in the air. There are only two of us.' We act like there are ten of us."

"That'd be lying."

"No. That the truth. There's you, me, your girlfriend, your nephew, and...and, the kid in the blue Taurus. And my brother Humberto."

"That's not ten, and your brother is in Mexico City."

"He give me advice all the time."

"I haven't received his bill."

"He work real cheap."

"I'm just a small PI with a zero-bedroom apartment for an office."

"I make message for your answering machine."

"What about your accent?"

"We're a global company."

"Excuse me, Garcia, I have to have a telecommunication with the Mayor of Randolph."

"You do good, chief. You use big words. That's good."

Milkey activated his cell phone.

"Mr. Gonzalez, this is Don Milkey. You wanted to talk to me?"

"Yes. I know you worked with John Friend, and, as I understand it, he had a bunch of violations, too."

"Yes."

"I've been trying get rid of these records, but the system won't allow it. They get flushed by paperwork. Either I have to pay the fine, or appear in court, and the paperwork generated by those two actions will allow them to be deleted. Did Friend have the same problem?"

"I don't know, but I suspect he did."

"Well, it's ruining my life, Milkey. I carry a letter around with me from a Judge that says there's been an error, but that's not enough. When I go into a different jurisdiction, I get pulled over, and my troubles start again. Also, I'm getting more violations. Yesterday, I got a seventy in a fifty. The letter doesn't mention that. To make matters worse, I tried to withdraw an investment I made awhile ago, and they won't let me do it. I got twenty-thousand in a bank that won't let go of it. I know you don't want to know all these details, but my life is shit with all these violations. I think it's affected my credit in some way."

"What do they say is the problem with the twenty-thousand?"

"It's got some sort of lien or demand on it. They can't let it go until it's resolved. Can you help me on this?"

"I can."

"I don't have much money to pay you, but when this is resolved, I can."

"Don't worry, I'll do what I can for you. I'll be in touch."

Chapter 66

"Hello. Miss Schmidt? This is Brent Iverson with Innovative Software Solutions in Denver. I haven't been able to return my calls. I've been submerged in a new software launch. Are you a business writer for the Star?"

"No, I'm an investigative reporter for our local news."

"Oh?"

"Mr. Iverson, I'm doing some investigation into the case of John Friend, a local police chief who was killed."

"Yes?"

"Well...your name came up in my research."

"Hmm."

"I...thought you might want to comment."

"No. Don't know the guy."

"Do you know a guy by the name of Don Milkey?"

"Can't say I remember the name."

"Cassidy?"

"What?"

"Cassidy. Do you know someone named Cassidy?"

"His name doesn't come to mind."

"He's a captain with the Kansas City, Missouri police department."

"I've been fortunate enough not to know any police officers."

"Does your company have any business in Kansas City?"

"No."

"You don't know John Friend."

"I've met a lot of people in the security business. I don't remember all of their names."

"If I may, Mr. Iverson, my sources seemed to think you are important in this case."

"Who are your sources?"

"Don Milkey."

"Don't know the guy."

"Mr. Iverson, when I mentioned the subject of my investigation, the death of John Friend, you only had a one word response."

"So?"

"So, if I was in your shoes, and a stranger, a reporter from a large midwest newspaper called me about the death of a police chief, I would immediately ask, 'why are you calling me?'"

"I don't understand."

"You weren't curious about my subject."

"So?"

"So. My subject has come across your desk before, and therefore you have not been truthful with me, right?"

Brent did not respond.

"Mr. Iverson. Right?"

Chapter 67

"Hi, Portia, this is Don."

"Hello, are you getting any farther with the case?"

"I am. I need to ask you a few questions about John."

"Go ahead."

"Was he trying to straighten out all the violations that appeared on his record?"

"Oh, my yes. It consumed him. He thought a police chief could just go in and wipe the records out, but it wasn't as easy as that. He spent days working through that."

"Did he handle the money in your family?"

"Yes, he did. He made out the budget, and he invested our money. He was good at that, not me."

"At any time during his dealing with these bad records, did he ever mention any money problems?"

Portia paused. Milkey waited.

"Mr. Milkey, I really don't know our finances. We always seemed to have enough. We ate out a lot. Not fancy restaurants, not fast food, though. I read the mail. If we were in trouble, I'd have seen it there. But there is one thing I should tell you about, that I promised myself I wouldn't talk about. I didn't right off know that it was connected with his death, so I didn't say anything about it. The afternoon I came back to my empty house after his funeral, I didn't know what to do, but what I usually do in the afternoon, clean the kitchen. When I tossed some paper into the trash can, I saw some coffee grounds poured into the trash. They were unused grounds. I looked into the cupboard where we keep our coffee. The coffee can was gone. I looked through the rest of the cupboards and found it next to our tea and sugar. I pulled it down off the shelf. I shook it, but I heard nothing. It was fairly light, as if it was empty. I opened it. There was a note on top in John's handwriting. It said: 'this is ours, keep it safe.' Beneath the note was nineteen thousand, seven hundred dollars in cash. It's now nineteen two, I'm paying you from the can. I hope I haven't kept some important information from you."

"I don't see right now how it fits in. But it's unusual. I'd like to see your financial records, if you don't mind."

"No problem."

Chapter 68

Beep.

"Pick up the phone, Don. Do it. Just lift up the receiver and put it to your ear. I know you're there. Come on, honey. This is important. I'm dying. I could be dead by the time you call me back. Okay, I was kidding about dying. I'm leaving you if you don't pick up the phone right now. That'll teach you. Oh, wait, that won't. Just pick up the fucking phone."

"Hello?"

"Well Christ on a bike, you picked up."

"You threatened me."

"That's too harsh. I pointed out consequences."

"What's so important?"

"I just wanted to know if you knew where Lulu was."

"That's important?"

"Yeah, the lady who brought you Rathbone? She's important for what she did for you, besides being a human being."

"The answer is: I don't know."

"Don't you worry about her?"

"Sure. But, you might review the history. It appears she doesn't need anyone to protect her from the perils of being homeless."

"And what about Rathbone?"

"What about him?"

"Where is he?"

"I don't know."

"Don't you care about him? Where he's sleeping? Where he's getting his food?"

"I do."

"Well?"

"He doesn't want to be found. Therefore, I'm not looking for him."

"And Jake."

"Put your coffee down, Helen."

"How did you know I was drinking coffee?"

"You're on a rant. I'd say you're on your third cup."

"It's decaffinated."

"I don't think so."

"It's got a...green label. Wait a minute, I can prove it."

"Jake helped me last time I talked to Rathbone."

"Oh, honey."

"Rathbone was impressed. He thought Jake was in college."

"Don. He's seventeen. His mother worries about him."

"He's got a chance to make a difference in someone's life, Helen. Yeah, he's young. He's smart. He's got a talent that will help Rathbone and Portia. There is a risk for him. I'll try to minimize the risk. I'll just do my best."

"Have you described the white van to him?"

"The blue van."

"Jesus, they've got another one?"

"Yes."

"Just be careful, Don. I worry. You know that's my job. I worry about everyone, including Garcia."

"He's..." Milkey stopped.

"He's what?"

"Nothing."

"What, what's happened to Garcia? Something's happened. Tell me."

"It was nothing."

"Don."

"He got roughed up. He's fine. It was just a message they were sending. He's okay."

"Ah, geez, honey. Couldn't you learn to lie to me? Just once. Try it. Let's practice. Was it the guys in the blue van?"

"No, it was a jilted woman. She smacked him all over the place."

"Thank you, Don. I knew you could do it. I feel much better now."

Chapter 69

"Your husband kept a record of everything?" Helen asked.

"He was very detailed. Everything had its place," Portia said.

"Everything but the twenty thousand."

"I know. It wasn't like him. We had a checking account, a savings account, some IRA's and some other investments. But, he never had a coffee can, until the last days of his life."

"I went through his checkbook and I couldn't see anything written for twenty thousand, or even ten."

"We paid cash for things. He carried about five hundred around with him wherever he went."

"I checked the credit card. Again, no large transaction."

"He rarely used it, except for travel."

"I see his trip to St. Louis. Hotel and conference fees."

"Yes, they would be repaid by the department."

"They were."

"In the folder for investments, he's got mutual funds, which are all IRA's, an indexed mutual fund at Vanguard. And here's a folder titled 'Silver Shield'. What's that?"

"I don't know."

"It's got what appears to be an application. It's hand written. There's nothing else in the folder. It looks like a purchase of a certificate of deposit, for twenty thousand."

"He never told me about that."

"There's handwritten notes all over the inside of the folder. Dates. Phone calls made. There's a lot of activity here. It looks like he invested in a CD, and he's called one guy about fifteen times. Portia, I need to do some research on these funds. This is the only place I find a recent large transaction. The vanguard and IRA funds don't have any recent paperwork. That means they're online. Are the passwords in these folders?"

"I've got a separate list. I never got into the funds. But John made sure I had passwords in case something happened to him. I've checked the accounts, and there doesn't seem to be anything out of the ordinary, except the Vanguard fund is empty."

"I know I'm asking you to trust me," Helen said. "This is a big thing. I've got all your passwords for your financial accounts."

"Don't think nothing about it. I asked Mr. Milkey if I could trust you. He said yes."

"That's great, but how come you trust Don?"

"That's easy, hon. I know the judge don't lie."

Chapter 70

"Thornton, I don't understand why we just don't turn off the phones, turn out the lights and head out to the Bahamas."

"Because we got money in banks, Iverson."

"So? We just transfer it to an off-shore account."

"We can't have nine million sitting in a bank when the shit hits the fan."

"Why not? They're offshore. They're not in our names."

"The plan stands, Iverson. We're forced to end the project early, but we'll follow the wind-down plan that was already in place. The way we disrupt the paper trail is to unload the accounts into cash. That means we milk the ATM's for small amounts until the electronic digits are gone."

"That's going to take time."

"We've got to do it. We can never destroy the evidence, but we can make it so complicated, no one will be able to come after us."

"You've done this before."

"Sure."

"You've never been caught."

"I've been caught every time."

"What? You didn't tell me this when we first met."

"It's nothing. I was caught twelve years ago. They're still trying to make the case. I'll get caught here, and I'll be dead before the jury comes in."

"What about me?"

"You'll be caught, too."

"What do I do?"

"Hah. You call me, and I'll give you the name and number of a good lawyer. You keep a small fund you'll use to slow it all down. You'll be surprised how easy it is. That's why we liquidate our assets into unmarked cash."

"You got a big stash, Thornton?"

"From other deals, yes."

"How much?"

"Enough."

"Where do you keep it?"

"In many places. I've got some in my wallet right now."

"Sounds risky."

"Risky? I'll tell you what's risky. A nine-million dollar bank account in Timbuktu National Bank in the Fiji Islands, that's what's risky. If you don't understand anything about this end plan, understand this: we're taking our hard earned money off the grid. Sure, we won't make interest on the money, but no one will ever know where it is, and how much it is. That's the beauty of the plan."

"What about John Friend?"

"What about him?"

"He's dead."

"That would be one less witness. Wouldn't that be good?"

"It makes it more than stealing money."

"Don't go ethical on me, Iverson."

"You don't worry about Friend?"

"No, I worry about Milkey."

Chapter 71

"Want some coffee?"

Don and Helen sat at the kitchen table in the home of Samuel Bolin. Barking dogs, auto carcasses, and a shotgun pointing at the ground had greeted them at the modest manufactured house ten miles out of Bolivar, Missouri.

"No, thanks," said Don.

"Ma'am?"

"I've already had too much this morning. Thank you," Helen said.

"Henry told me about what you doin' for a coupla guys up there in Kansas City. He's my brother-in-law an' he's a Mexican, but that don't make no never mind to me. Color man's skin, don' have anything to do with the color of a man's heart, ya understand?"

"Mr. Bolin, we've talked with Henry, and he seems to be in a real bind."

"Now folks, y'all call me Sammy, that's what folk 'round here call me."

"Sammy, have you had trouble with traffic violations?" Helen asked.

"Oh yeah. Got a shit pile of 'em. But that's no big deal around these parts. I see you got a Vic, too. Mine's a police intro-cepta, and it don' take much to get up to 95, even on the gravel roads. Me and the sheriff have a deal. If those tickets get to overflowin,' I just sell a hog or two, and donate to a fund of his likin'. Deep down, I'm a charitable guy. Sheriff, he appreciates that."

"So the tickets aren't a concern to you?"

"No ma'am. It's the damn twenty thousand that's got my scivies up a crack."

"You had twenty thousand invested, just like Henry."

"That's right. I got that money fair and square, an' I'm not partial to givin' it up to some fancy talker in a suit. Got that money when I got hit by the UPS truck an' killed my huntin' dog 'shitforbrains.' No, he was dumb as a dildo, pardon my french, ma'am, but he could track. Ooo boy, could he track. He was worth forty, but I took twenty. Pain and suferrin', ya know."

"Where did you invest the money?"

"Same place as Henry. It was to get eighteen per cent, that lyin' mother said. Hell, now we got zero, Henry an' me."

"Was it a CD?"

"Yeah, it was. I called 'em wantin' to get my money out. But they said, 'no sir', imagine that. They called me 'sir' while they screwed me."

"What did they say was the reason why you couldn't get it out?"

"They said I had to wait six months 'fore I could take it out. Ah said I'd be down in six minutes with my best friend, Buckshot."

"Where is the CD?"

"Oh, hell, I don' remember, some bank out in Bumfuck, Kansas."

"You went all the way to Kansas to buy a CD?"

"Nah, didn't Henry tell you? We got these sum-biches in St. Louis at the convention. I'm regional director of security for Quintin's Quick Stores hereabouts. I try to keep up on the latest word in methods and tech-i-nology."

"You bought them at the convention?"

"Well, some did, some just wrote a check. I didn't have that in my bank. When I got home I wired it to that skunk."

"Who was it?"

"Don't remember the name. He was like a preacher. He was a sweet talker, and he promised us 18% and a ticket to heaven, by God. Henry wrote out a check and handed it to him. I said, Henry, ya' got that money in the bank? He say yeah. When I got back home, I thought twice 'bout it. But that greasy little skunk called me, and called me Sammy, like he knew me, and he remembered the scar on my face, this one right above my eye, and he thought that racoon probably got the worst of it, and said he didn't believe Henry when Henry said it was a woman who did it. He was slicker than snot on

Sunday, he was. I transferred twenty to bumfuck bank in Salina, Kansas, I think it was."

"Did this guy have a booth at the convention?"

"Booth? Hell, he had the whole stage. He was a presenter. He was on the agenda, 'How to Make Your Money Work For You' the program said. He sold them like selling beads to Catholics."

"Who did this guy work for?"

"I don't know. Maybe the bank. Maybe some other business. At the time, it seemed like he was working for the Lord, hisself. Now, I call him a skunk because of what he did to me and Henry. But he smelled like a whore, dressed like one, had a fancy tie and suit on, and one more thing that should have said 'whoa' to me: ya ain't gonna believe this, but he had hair the color of the Ace of Spades, and it had a white streak down the middle, no lie."

Chapter 72

In the back of Molly B's, two men and a teenager sat in discussion.

"We didn't know how to get in touch with you," Milkey said.

"That would be the point," Rathbone said.

"Do you know where Lulu is?"

"Yes."

"Is she okay?"

"Yes."

"Why did you want Jake and I to come down here?"

"I have a problem I can't figure out; it won't let go of me. Jake, if you use multiple operating systems to get around the three-request limit, how do you switch them? Surely you don't reboot every three tries."

"I don't know how it does it, but it doesn't reboot. I think it's a Unix system running a program that simulates the other operating systems."

"That would be impossible to do. That would be like re-inventing Windows 7 and XP and all of the others."

"If it does simulate them, I figure they'd just be barebones control. That would be possible."

"Is there any way I could take a look at it?"

"Sure," Jake said, pushing his laptop over to Rathbone. "Try my yahoo mail."

"How do I kick it off?"

"Type in anything for user and password. You'll get a popup."

"Ah, guys, if I may interrupt," Milkey said.

"Yeah sure, go ahead," Rathbone said as he typed.

"The guy who is the head of marketing at Innovative Solutions."

"Yeah?"

"What does he sell?"

"What's your street number?"

"671, but it ain't gonna work," Jake said.

"What does he sell?" Milkey asked.

"Software," Rathbone said. "What now?"

"Well, you know it has Jake in it. If you looked on my facebook page, you'd find the name of my dog, my favorite computer game. It's already up, check it out."

"He doesn't sell investments?"

"Who?"

"Paul Mazzoli, your vice-president of marketing."

"What about him."

"Listen, Jake, Kevin. Pay attention. Sammy Bolin, a guy down in Bolivar invested twenty thousand dollars with a guy who presented at the Security Convention in St. Louis. His brother-in-law did too. They can't get their money out. The guy who hawked the investment was a salesman with black hair and a white streak down the middle. The investment was a CD from a bank in Salina, Kansas. Does any of this mean anything to you, Kevin?"

Rathbone leaned back in his chair. "Just the streak."

"Not the bank?"

"No. Our customers were in Wyoming and Colorado. And I think they were bringing one on board in Scotts Bluff, Nebraska."

Jake pulled his laptop back over to his side of the table.

"But, Paul would have called on just about every bank in Colorado and western Kansas."

"Is he a good salesman?"

"Ice cubes to Eskimos good."

"Which bank in Salina was it, Uncle Don?"

"I'm not sure."

"I'm looking at Bank of the Plains. I see a little logo on the sign in page."

"Let's see that," said Rathbone as he pulled the laptop over to himself. Yes, they're in. That's the Smart Shield logo, down there in the lower right hand of the screen."

"You never heard of Paul selling anything else than software."

"No, but I did notice that he talked about going to Omaha and Kansas City, and I think, St. Louis. The original plan was the states touching Colorado, but I thought maybe he just went beyond that on his own."

"The guy in St. Louis with the black and white hair, selling CD's from a bank in Salina, Kansas, one that is a customer of yours...that pretty well pins it down to Innovative Solutions, don't you think? Don asked.

"I'm in," Rathbone said. "You've got an email from someone in Nigeria offering you three million dollars."

"How long did it take?" Jake asked.

"About five minutes. Was it using different operating systems?"

"You really can't tell. There is a log produced by the utility, but I've never used it."

"I'm in awe, Jake. God I wish I had my laptop."

Jake looked at his uncle. Then he reached down into his backpack and pulled out a small computer. "Would it be all right if Mr. Rathbone used my netbook, uncle Don?"

"It's your computer, Jake."

"I mean, you might worry about security and all."

"I think Dr. Rathbone will be careful."

Chapter 73

"Mr. Johnson, a Mr. Milkey is here to see you." The receptionist looked at Milkey's business card. "He's a private investigator from the firm of Milkey, Stosberg, Garcia and Jackson in Kansas City."

A tall man, in suit and tie, approached Don in the vestibule of the Bank.

"What brings you to Salina this morning, Mr. Milkey."

"I'm researching some investments made by my clients in Certificate of Deposits in your bank."

"I'm not sure I can talk about my customers. That would be a breach of confidence."

"Their names are Henry Gonzales and Samual Bolin."

"I don't recognize the names, but we have over twenty-thousand customers here in central Kansas. But, even if I did, I couldn't talk about them."

"They each invested twenty thousand in CD's at your bank, and now they can't get them out."

"Sometimes there are introductory periods when it'd not be smart to cash them out early because of the penalty for doing so."

"No, these can't be cashed out at any penalty."

"That would surprise me."

"Mr. Johnson, do you work with a company called Innovative Solutions?"

Johnson stared at Milkey. He picked up Milkey's business card and dialed the number.

"Mr. Stosberg, please." He pressed the receiver closer to his ear. "Oh, I'm sorry, Miss Stosberg. Helen? Okay. What? Say that again? I see. No. No message. Thank you."

Johnson turned to Milkey. "Your receptionist has such a thick accent, I couldn't understand him very well."

"We're a global company."

"Innovative Solutions, Mr. Milkey? I'm sorry, but we're going to have to end our meeting without resolving your clients' problem. "

"Something wrong?"

"Yes, frankly. Innovative Solutions provides us with security for our customer accounts. They are very good. They also advise us on physical, and on-site breaches of security. In fact, just yesterday I got a call from Mr. Iverson at Innovative Solutions alerting me to the possibility of someone showing up at our bank with some customer complaints as a way to break into our system. They are very professional, Mr. Milkey."

"You think I'm a threat?" Milkey asked.

"I'm not saying you are, but, as a result of Mr. Iverson's advice, we've implemented some on-site procedures. Maybe you saw the off-duty policeman at the door. He greeted you, for sure."

"Yes, he did. But you have to also be aware of other security problems you have."

"Like what?"

"A third-party software company coming in and loading their product on your system and then stealing your customers' money."

"Ha. That's exactly the story Iverson said was going around. He told me that you, or someone else, had been to three other banks with the same cockamamie story. That's how good this Innovative Solutions is. Johnson pressed a button. "Linda, please send officer McNulty in here."

"Mr. Johnson, you're sure no money has left your bank that you don't know about?"

"Mr. Milkey, I know your profession is private investigation, so you don't know much about accounting. We start with X dollars at the beginning of the day, we add receipts and subtract disbursements, and we have Y dollars at the end of the day. We have accounting control over this."

"And each transaction identifies the source of the transaction."

"No source, no transaction. That's how the system works."

"I wouldn't bet the farm on it, Mr. Johnson."

Chapter 74

"Care for some coffee, Garcia?" Don asked. "Helen?"

No response came from the other two people at Milkey's kitchen table.

"I'd like one of those cinnamon crisps, honey."

"I don't have any."

"I'd still like to have one."

"Maybe Jackson has some."

"Nah, that's okay, I'll just sit here with nothing."

"Maybe you could fry up some," Garcia said.

"I have no cinnamon."

"No cinnamon, no coffee, what do you have, boss."

"Tea. I got tea. Og-gal-log tea, black tea, green tea."

"You so California, boss."

"I got those for his birthday."

"This year?"

"No."

"Friend wrote a check the last day of the convention."

"Oh?"

"Yeah, I got it right here. It was cashed at the Salina High Plains bank the next day. It came from a Vanguard mutual fund account. Gonzales told me that was the same bank his check was cashed at. I'm sure the same with Sammah."

"Sammy?"

"No, Sammah. Both checks were written to Wind River Investments. Friend has a receipt signed by a Paul Mazzoli."

"Sixty thousand dollar, Boss. That not much."

"But we determined about fifty people had the same ticket problems as these three guys," Helen said.

"That'd be a million," Don said. "I suspect it's more."

"Million not enough boss?"

"For us, yes, but for Innovative Solutions, it'd be just a start. Garcia, the blue van, does it have Maryland license plates?"

"Yes."

"Are they the same people?"

"Not sure boss. I didn't get good look at face with fist in stomach."

Chapter 75

"Come into my office, would you, Mr. Milkey?"

Don took a seat across from Sandra Schmidt at the newspaper office.

"You talked to Iverson?" Don asked.

"Yes, I told him I was writing a story that implicated him and his company in investment fraud. That he installed software in a bank, investments were directed to the bank, and the software removed it and covered it up."

"What'd he say?"

"He didn't. His chief of security, Thornton Hopkins came on the phone and told me I was investigating matters of national security. He said he couldn't say much about it, but that Innovative Solutions was contracted by the NSA to implement and test a security system in several banks in the Midwest. He asked me to delay any publication so that the project could run its course. He leaned on my patriotism."

"You believed him?"

"I don't believe any one, Milkey, including you. I have to confirm everything I write."

"Who confirms the NSA connection?"

"That would be the NSA."

"Haa, how convenient. Let me guess, you couldn't find anyone at NSA to confirm Thornton's project."

"No."

"Or deny?"

"Or deny."

"Have you checked me out?"

"Yes."

"With who?"

"Cassidy, for one."

"What'd he say?"

"He said you're a liar, and would say anything for money."

"What'd he say about the email in Iverson's trash can quoting him that "I was too dumb to worry about?"

"He said anyone could create an email saying anything. It wasn't proof. I need something more, Milkey. I just can't go on your word."

"Maybe you'd like to talk to Kevin Rathbone."

"Who's he?"

"He was the team leader of the project for Innovative Solutions, until he left under threat of his life."

Chapter 76

Sunday morning, about 9:00, the back table of Molly B's bar and grill.

"I'm not sure I can talk for publication," said Kevin.

"After I write it, you can read it, I promise," Schmidt said.

"Kevin, think what you can do for John Friend's wife," Helen said. "And all those people who have their investments in that bank in Salina."

"My life's in danger."

"Who is after you, Kevin?" Sandra asked.

"It would be the guys hired by Hopkins to find and silence me."

"Why would they want to do that?"

"Because I came across something in the program that I thought needed to be fixed."

"What needed to be fixed?"

"It was the identification model being used to distinguish a threat from an authorized entry. Wait a minute. Now I know why they wouldn't change it. They wanted access to accounts, and they wanted to lock out certain customers."

"So, they sold CD investments to guys at a security convention. Dumped them all into a bank in Salina." Helen said.

"And locked them all out," Milkey said.

"Where does John Friend enter the story?" Sandra asked.

"We don't have proof," Don said, "but I believe that it was in their plan that they would begin to have some backlash, some buyer's remorse. When John Friend started complaining, they entered violations into the database. His wife said that he was consumed with knocking down these violations. The same thing happened to Gonzalez and Bolin. Obviously, they were buying time to remove the funds from the bank."

"Why didn't they just take the money and run?" Sandra asked.

"It makes sense. They built a legitimate business, they sold software and investments. These are clever people. They know it's going to be discovered."

"All that for a paltry million dollars from fifty customers?" Helen asked.

"Nope," Kevin said. "A million is nothing to these guys. I see it now."

"What do you see?" Don asked.

"It's so beautiful."

"Share it with us," Helen said.

"It's not the CD funds they want. That's just a test. All of the other accounts in the banks are accessible by the software, too. They've got ten banks. Let's say they get an additional million from each of them plus the CD fund. That's eleven million."

"Now we're talking," Helen said.

Chapter 77

"What do you have, Jake?"

"You asked me to get into the Innovative Solutions system."

"Right."

"All they have is email."

"You don't see anything that indicates the development of Panther."

"No. But if I were them, I'd keep that activity on their own LAN in their office only. But I've got something from their email."

"Tell me."

"There are nine email addresses, including Kevin's. There is little, if any, activity going on. However, they are all set to out-of-office replies. This means they're not in the office much of the time, all of them. The email traffic among them occurs in the early evening. Furthermore, on one of the emails from Hopkins was an encrypted file."

"What was in the file."

"I couldn't translate it. But I could tell what's in it."

"What's in it?"

"I detected four fields of information in each of thirty-nine records. The first field

contained a recurring four-character string. The other three fields in each of the records had recurring strings. I just made a guess. There are forty banks in the Denver area. Bank accounts, a person's name, username and password...four fields."

"Do you know for sure?"

"Yep. I took the list of banks, and the list of employees at Innovative Solutions. I picked a bank at random, an employee at random, and a dollar amount at random. I called the banks telling them I needed to know if a check written for x amount of dollars on x's account would be covered. I made twenty calls, and got twenty responses that they would be covered."

"Jesus, their money is spread around the banks in Denver. What's the most in one account?"

"I did another twenty calls, this time increasing the dollar amount each call."

"And...?"

"There is a confusing variable in the research. The higher you go, the more likely the bank is going to invoke privacy policy. But there is an interesting pattern, as I went up the scale. For the receptionist at Innovative Solutions, the bank would say they could cover a 35,000 check, but not a 50,000 check. For Hopkins, they could cover 35,000, but at 50,000, they invoked their policy. To me, that was an affirmative response."

"What are they doing, Jake?"

"They've decentralized their money. That's what I would do. I wouldn't put the money in one offshore account. That would be too dangerous. I would put it in small local banks, many of them."

"Sounds inefficient."

"It would be hard to detect."

"It would be a prelude to their next step."

"And that would be...?"

"Using ATM's to take their money out of the banking system."

Chapter 78

Don Milkey opened the door to his apartment. He stood in the doorway, looking into the darkness.

"Mr. Hopkins," Milkey said.

There was no reply.

"Thornton Hopkins?" Milkey repeated.

"Mr. Milkey."

Don turned the light on. Sitting in Don's recliner with a .38 pistol on the end table was Thornton Hopkins, chief of security for Innovative Solutions.

"How did you know I was here?" Hopkins asked.

"I saw your car parked on the street."

"You don't know the car I drive."

"I saw a Mercedes 340SL. No one around here drives that kind of car."

"This is a questionable neighborhood, Mr. Milkey. There are drug dealers around here no doubt."

"You're too far from the street, Hopkins. No drug dealer drives an SL."

Don entered the room and shut the door.

"Well maybe some rich guy with taste is visiting a friend in the apartment building."

"Hopkins, I'm the only one here that would know someone who could afford a 340SL. And among the people I know, only two would drive that kind of car, you and Iverson. I ruled out Iverson because he wouldn't have the guts to come here. Therefore, I knew it was you."

"Clever, Milkey. And that's the reason I'm here. If I may, we share a talent. We both have a different look on the generalities of life, but we're in the same profession."

"What profession is that?"

"Information."

"Could you slim it down a bit?"

"Sure. You're able to take a whole shit-pile of information and narrow it down to its essence."

"And we're alike in that manner?"

Milkey looked at the pistol on the end table. Hopkins picked it up and placed it in a holster under his sport jacket.

"Oh no. I'm the one who builds the shit-pile. That's our connection."

"Let's see if I can make this concrete," Milkey said. "You want to steal money from people, but instead of using a gun, you use an investment vehicle to get them to put money in a bank which you rob silently with modern-day technology."

"I've never been a favorite of the concrete," Hopkins said. "Shit-pile is as close as I can come."

"Like the load of cash you have in the trunk of your SL."

Hopkins eyebrows lifted. "I'm curious, Milkey. Who did your hacking? I know it wasn't you, and Rathbone wouldn't stoop that low. Who was it?"

"I googled 'hacker' on the internet. Got one real cheap in India."

"I'm sure you did, Milkey, but I prefer to think he's someone you know. I'm guessing the guy has never seen the inside of a graduate program, let alone a university. He's a kid, isn't he? He taught himself."

Milkey didn't reply.

"And that's how we're the same, Milkey, you know I have cash in my trunk, and I know who your hacker is, and no one told us."

"What about Friend?"

"What about what?"

"John Friend. My client's husband who was shot dead on the interstate."

"Oh, John Friend. You need to take that up with the authorities."

"I have. They won't do anything about it."

"That's too bad. I'm sorry for you and your client."

"I don't think you are. I think John Friend was just a cost of doing business to you."

"That's what I like about you, Milkey. You read people. You read people well. That puts us in a tiny group together. We share that ability. You can't escape it."

Milkey turned around at the sound of a knock on the door. He opened it.

"Mr. Milkey, I assembled the operations team," Garcia said, looking past Don at the visitor.

"Oh?"

"I have seven men ready."

"Seven?"

"Yes, sir."

"Stand your team down, Garcia."

"Yes, Mr. Milkey, we stand down."

Don shut the door.

"It must be nice," said Hopkins, "to have your associates live and work at your apartment building."

Milkey said nothing.

"And your girlfriend must help you out quite a lot."

Hopkins leaned forward in the chair.

"Milkey, I know you pretty well. I'm going to leave your apartment in a few minutes.

You're not going to stop me. You could accompany me to my car where I would offer you a million dollars in unmarked, untraceable twenties so that you would end your case right now. Prove me right. You wouldn't take the money, would you?"

"Now there you're wrong, Hopkins. I would take the money and end the case."

"You would?"

"Certainly. Here's what I'd do. I'd take the million in cash to Portia Friend. I would ask her if she wanted the money or your ass in jail. Now, you don't know her, so you need some information in order to know her decision. I'll give you a short history: John Friend grew up in New Orleans, Louisiana, where he saw his family and friends treated like shit by the police. He became a policeman and rose up through the ranks to become the first black chief of police in this area. He worked long hours and bad hours, sometimes not seeing his wife for days. A reason he was successful is because of the support and sacrifice of his wife. Now I ask you, which will she chose? A million dollars or your ass in jail?"

"I've got to be going, Milkey. It was nice talking to you. You don't need to see me out."

Hopkins stood up and put his gun away. He offered Milkey his hand to shake.

"Save your hand for the cuffs," said Don.

"You're not going to arrest me. You're just a private eye."

"That's right."

"But you believe justice will be served."

"Yes."

"How will that happen?"

"Karma."

"Oh come on, Milkey, you're tarnishing my image of you."

"I see the future."

"And karma is there?"

"Yup."

Chapter 79

Milkey stood on the balcony overlooking the street where the Mercedes was parked. A three-hundred-pound Latino male sat on the hood of the SL. The front of the car leaned toward the ground. Six other people from his neighborhood surrounded the car. They all wore blue KC Royals caps. Garcia leaned against a car behind the Mercedes.

Hopkins strode towards his car. Garcia stepped in front of him. During the five minute conversation, Hopkins said nothing. Garcia signaled his men; they left. Hopkins got into his SL and sped off.

"You didn't need to do that, Garcia."
"I need to."
"You put yourself in danger."
"I don't take chance."
"Who's the big guy?"
"My cousin, Humberto."
"I thought he was in Mexico City."
"He was. He now in Kansas City for holiday."
"What did you say to Hopkins."
"I say, 'no come back'."
"Seems like you said more than three words."
"Sometimes my poor English, I have to say many words."
"Do you think he understood you?"
"Yes."
"How do you know? He didn't say anything."
"I no need words. I see his eyes."
"Eyes?"

"When he come up to me his eyes say he angry. When I talk to him, his eyes say he scared. He not come back."

"He was armed. Did you know that?"

"Yes. I not afraid. Humberto, he big, not slow."

"Thanks for your help, Garcia, although you put yourself at risk there."

"I good dick, Chief?"

Milkey looked down at the ground, then back to Garcia.

"You good friend."

Garcia flung his arms around Milkey.

"Don't worry, Chief. I happy. I not gay."

Chapter 80

Milkey opened his laptop on the table in the back of Molly B's. A glass of ice water sweated near the mousepad. He was typing when Dr. Rathbone walked up.

"Jackson said I'd find you here."

"I have several offices," Don said. "Can I buy you a drink?"

"At ten in the morning? No thanks."

"Where have you been hiding?"

"At a small church in the River Market area. They take in a few of the homeless guys. They feed us, and we do a little work around the place."

"You're not accustomed to that kind of work, I'll bet."

"You'd be surprised. It's a change. I didn't mind it."

"I've talked to Hopkins."

"You went to Denver?"

"No, he came here."

"What?"

"Yup."

"Was he looking for me?"

"He didn't mention you. He said it was a professional visit."

"What'd he want?"

"I'm not sure. He said he and I were in the same business."

"Hardly."

"I think he prides himself on his knowledge of security."

"He does. He didn't try to get information on me?"

"He didn't."

"Could I borrow your phone?"

"Sure."

Rathbone punched in a phone number. After a few minutes, he said, "no response."

"Are they open at this time?"

"It's nine a.m in Denver. They should answer or at least send me to voice mail."

"What does that mean."

"It means they're gone. Voice mail was in the equipment. They've taken everything. That would explain Hopkin's visit."

"That makes sense."

" Milkey, could I use your phone again. I'd like to call my wife."

Rathbone went to the front of the bar to make his call. Milkey continued searching for keys on the keyboard.

"Have you seen Lulu?" Don asked when Rathbone returned.

"Yes." Kevin pulled a folded sealed envelope from his back pocket. "She wanted me to give you this. It's for Portia Friend. Lulu was leaving town, and if she needed you, she'd call."

"What are your plans?"

"I'm heading back to Denver. Thanks for keeping me safe, Mr. Milkey."

"Lula did the work. I hope you thanked her."

"I did. But she found some reason to trust you. That's on you."

Milkey finished his typing and pressed "send."

Chapter 81

"Mr. Milkey, you've got something for me?" Sandra Schmidt asked.

Don Milkey sat comfortably in a chair in an office in the *Kansas City Star* building.

"I do. I've written a report to Portia Friend. It's the result of my investigation of the murder of her husband. I'd like you to have a copy."

"Will our readers find it interesting?"

"No they won't. It has a few loose ends."

"Like what?"

"Like Captain Cassidy of the KCMO police department who refused, for personal gain, to investigate a murder."

The report rested in Milkey's lap. It was about two inches thick.

"You want me to tie up that loose end?"

"When you go to the police department, talk to Chief Kemp first. Tell him what you're doing."

"Why's that?"

"Out of courtesy to the department."

"What if he won't let me talk to Cassidy?"

"Use your own judgment after that."

Don handed her the report.

"What else?"

"At the end of the report is a list of phone numbers of those involved. I've written a note authorizing them to talk to you. Interview anyone you want. Track any lead. Don't worry about offending someone."

"In other words, act like you."

"You wouldn't go wrong."

Chapter 82

Milkey sat in his recliner and sipped from a cup of coffee. He pressed the 'play' button on his voice mail machine.

Beep.

Mr. Milkey, this is Portia. Sandra Schmidt from the Star called me and asked a lot of questions. I told her what I knew. She was quite persistent, and she said she was working on your story, filling out the details. I didn't hold back. Hope I didn't screw anything up."

Click.

Beep.

"Hi, Don. Frank here. Haven't seen you at the meetings for quite some time. Hope everything is all right. Just called to say that God loves you, and so do I."

Click.

Beep.

"Don, this is Jeanne. I just finished the story in the papers this morning. I had no idea. And...and...I just wanted to thank you. There was no mention of Jake or even a description of him. I'm so proud of you both."

Click.

Beep.

"Mr. Milkey, this is Fry Collections calling about an unpaid invoice from Easy Ed's printing. Please call back so we can take care of this serious matter before it impacts your credit rating."

Click.

Beep.

"You son-of-a-bitch, Milkey, no wonder you couldn't cut it on the force. You got no loyalty or camaraderie. You send some bitch into my office asking questions that no one should be asking a policeman. You got no respect for authority. Don't call me next time someone mugs you on the street you asshole."

Click.

Beep.

"Mr. Milkey, this is Sarah Kline at the police department in Kearney. I thought you might like to know, we've got a police report in from Pueblo, Colorado. Their patrol stopped a Thornton Hopkins in a Mercedes. He was shot and wounded in an apparent attempt to flee. They found a large container of cash in the trunk of the car."

Click.

Beep.

"Don, pick up the phone. Do it. You can do it. Just lift up the receiver. Oh, okay. Hey I just wanted to tell you they've got a special going on down at city hall on marriage licenses. How 'bout you and I doing some shopping together? Loved your story."

Chapter 83

"Good morning, chief," Jackson said from his chair at the register.

"How you hanging, Jackson?" Milkey replied.

"Great story."

"Thanks. You must have been part of it."

"I was. I tried to keep my mouth shut, but hard to say no to a pretty woman like that."

"Persuasive."

"I don't know what you call it, but she was in my face something fierce. She didn't take 'I don't know' for an answer."

"It must have been hell for you."

"Thas' right, cap'm, and that perfume, it overcame me."

"Got any almond coffee?"

"What you want?"

"Almond flavored coffee."

"Cap'm, I got almonds and I got coffee. But they in different aisles. See, this how it works. I got a coffee aisle and a candy and nuts aisle. They ain't in the same place."

"Jackson, you only have three aisles. How come you call the coffee aisle the coffee aisle when it's got toilet paper in it, too?"

"There you go again, Milkey, thinkin' you're in the Piggly Wiggly."

"Looks like I'll just have to buy the plain old Folgers, old style."

"Worse things happen here in the ghetto, cap'm.

"That's why I shop at your store, Jackson. You're always lifting my spirits."

"Well lift me about five sixty-five out of your wallet for that coffee can."

"Here's a ten. Can you afford the change?"
Jackson held the bill up to the light and scrutinized it.
"My money no good here?"
"Just making sure it's got all its parts. Have a nice day, now."
Milkey opened the door to leave. He paused.
"What's up, cap'm."
"I was just waiting for you to say something."
"Like what?"
"Like what you usually say."
"What's that?"
"You usually ask if I'm your PI."
"Cap'm, I don't be asking things I already know the answer."
"Makes sense."
"Thas' why I never ask you if you my friend."
Milkey smiled and left the store.

Chapter 84

The man stood six inches from Milkey, shouting into his face.

"Milkey, I'm suspended because of you. You gave your guesses to the *Star*, and now I'm on leave from the force."

"Just doing my job, Cassidy."

A police cruiser entered the parking lot outside Jackson's store.

"You low-life PI, I'm wearing civilian clothes because of you. You don't know shit about evidence."

Spit flew out of Cassidy's mouth, some of it landing on Milkey's face.

"You're a moron. You're an asshole. You're going to regret this," Cassidy said.

Milkey stood steady in front of the barrage. A uniformed policeman emerged from the police car and walked over to the two men. Milkey glanced at the approaching young man. Cassidy continued without noticing the third man. The uniform was spotless. His shoes shined, and his name tag was brilliant brass etched with the name "Doherty."

"What's the trouble?" Sean asked.

Cassidy stopped his tirade and discovered Doherty.

"You take your rookie ass outta here. I can handle this."

Turning to Milkey, Doherty asked, "What's going on here?"

"I was in the store, buying coffee, and when I came out, this gentleman accosted me."

"I should've just leveled you, Milkey."

"Sir, I'm going to have to ask you to leave."

"He can't leave now, I'm not through with him," Cassidy said.

"No, sir, I mean you, Mr. Cassidy."

"Mister? You call me 'sir' or 'captain' or I'm going to put your career in a sling for insubordination."

"Mr. Cassidy, you are not an active member of the force. I do not report to you. I'm going to ask you, for the last time, get in your car and leave, or I will arrest you."

"You fuckin' pimply-faced kid. You don't know who you're dealing with. When I get back on the force, you'll be sorry you called me 'mister'."

"My car or your car, Mr. Cassidy."

Chapter 85

"Hope you weren't expecting chitlins and collard greens," Portia said as she placed the brisket on the table. "It's my anti-vegan meal. Hope you like it."

"It smells so good," Helen said. "Thanks for inviting us. If it were up to Don, we'd be celebrating at the Subway."

"Sandra Schmidt really did her work, didn't she?" Portia said.

"Don wrote a report, and she took it from there," Helen said. "I see there were two other guys arrested in addition to Hopkins."

"That Hopkins was shot just like John was. I wonder if he had multiple traffic violations?"

Don cut open a roll and buttered the inside.

"Don?" Helen said.

"What?"

"Did he have multiple violations?"

"Why would he have those? He was the perpetrator of that kind of hacking."

"Jake could do it, Don. Couldn't he?"

"He could."

"Did he?"

"No."

"Did you?"

"Pass the peas, please."

Portia, lifted the dish of peas and handed it to Don. "I don't care what you did, Mr. Milkey, or how you did it. We know how John was killed and who orchestrated it. I'm at peace now. I still miss John, but I'll live with that."

Don reached into his pocket and handed Portia the wrinkled envelope.

"Who's this from?" she asked.

"From Lulu," Don replied.

"Dear Mrs. Friend,

I ain't written anything in a coupla years, so you'll just have to figure out my handwritin' . And I had to make do with the paper. We don't have any stationery stores in my neighborhood. We don't even have a drugstore, at least one like Walgreens.

I know what you're thinkin' and feelin.' Cause I lost my husband, too. You're thinking if he'd left the house five minutes earlier or later, he'd still be with you. And, if the trooper had taken another half-second to decide, then you wouldn't be reading this letter.

That's how I felt when my husband was killed. I wish I could be there with you and hug you and tell you what I've learned the last coupla years. I can't. So you'll just have to read through my chicken scratches.

I learned fate and luck are on both sides. Those two boys had a decision to make, and not much time to make it. If your husband could talk, he'd say they did the right thing. They made the right decision. But fate and luck weren't with you that night. When that happened to me, I made a terrible decision to run away. I joined a group of people who did the same. Life is easy if the only choice you have is which street corner to stand on.

Mrs. Friend, it don't take much to matter. When I ran into Mr. Milkey in Jackson's store, I had a choice to stay or leave. I could tell he was a cop or at least was one time ago. In my life, cops is trouble. But, somethin' told me to stay. Maybe I was tired of leaving.

Believe this honey, when I talked to him, my life changed, and so did yours, girl. That little thing I did was a piece of a big puzzle, and a lot of lives were changed. Yup, your husband's not there, and you might think all you got is a letter in your hand, but you got more now. You got decisions to make, like we all do. If you don't make that decision because it seems too small, or too scary, or too different, you might as well come on down to the city and join the fellas who sleep next to the steam grate at 6th and Main. That's what they do. That's what I used to do.

You lost your husband, but you still got your choices. Make'em, girl. Your husband would be proud.

God bless you, if you're of that way of thinkin'.

Luellen Lucerne Frontenaire

Chapter 86

The cafe about six blocks from the Capitol Building in Topeka emptied out as 9:00 a.m. approached. The young man with the four-day beard remained behind, his stare fixed on the coffee cup in front of him. The bacon and eggs, half-eaten, grew cold on his table. The morning newspaper lay flat and unopened nearby. At a table in the back of the cafe sat a woman dressed in a dark business suit, sipping on her coffee. She opened her wallet and placed a few bills on the table, closed the wallet, pushed back her chair and stood up.

The young man did not look up as the woman strode directly towards him from the back table. Her heels tapped a strong and rhythmic beat. When she reached the table, the young man looked up.

"Officer Hendrix?" she asked.

"Yes?"

Her smile contradicted the tears forming in her eyes. Her hand moved forward and stretched out to the young man.

"I'm Portia Friend."

Dane Zeller

Smart Shield

ABOUT THE AUTHOR

Dane Zeller, is the author of *Drive-By Romances*, an anthology of romance stories gone wrong. He has published a number of humorous stories accessible through his web site, www.danezeller.com. He also teaches in the school of business at a university in Kansas City, Missouri.

Zeller lives with his wife in Westwood, Kansas

Also, by Dane Zeller:

Drive-By Romances
by
Dane Zeller

available at:
www.danezeller.com

15790551R00118

Made in the USA
Charleston, SC
20 November 2012